Halfway up the eastern wire my weight broke the crusty earth and one shoe slipped on the shoulder of something hard. I said: 'Wait'.

The soil came away under my fingers and I went on clearing it until they could define the shape. It was a curved shoulder and pitch-smooth and the detonator would be three or four inches to the right, in the centre. It would be at least a fourteen-ounce actuator, otherwise the odd crow or some heavy rainfall would trip it, so I finished the job and left the whole thing exposed.

'You shouldn't have done that.' His whisper was reedy with fright.

'You shouldn't have taken me so bloody close.'

ADAM HALL

The Striker
Portfolio

FONTANA BOOKS
BY AGREEMENT WITH
HEINEMANN

First published in Great Britain in 1969 by William Heinemann Ltd.
First issued in Fontana Books 1975

Copyright © Adam Hall 1969

Made and printed in Great Britain by
William Collins Sons & Co Ltd Glasgow

IN MEMORY OF MIKE

CONTENTS

Chapter One

THE FLY

'*Haben Sie sich verlaufen?*'

'*Ja, ich möchte nach Villendorf.*'

'*Es gibt keinen solchen Ort hier.*'

'*Vielleicht ist es Wohlendorf. Die Leute, die mir davon erzählten, hatten keine sehr gute Aussprache.*'

'*Wohlendorf – ah, ja! Das ist etwas ganz anderes. Aber es ist ziemlich weit von hier.*'

'*Vielleicht könnten Sie so freundlich sein, und es mir auf der Karte zu zeigen –* '

'*Ich kann nicht einmal Karten lesen. Aber Sie müssen zuerst nach Westheim fahren.*'

He pointed up the road.

'*Ich glaube, ich bin dort durchgefahren.*'

'*Sie müssen durchgefahren sein. Fahren Sie dorthin züruck und fragen Sie dann in Westheim.*'

I folded the map.

'*Ja, haben Sie vielen Dank.*'

He was old, a weather-stained man. He watched me turn the car; then in the mirror he was blotted out by the dust.

In two kilometres I took a small road south and turned again to come back parallel and stay in the area. It was routine procedure to tell him I had lost my way. Later it could prove to have been bad security to be seen in this area standing by a car doing nothing. He would remember a man losing his way but it was better than remembering a man standing by a car doing nothing.

But I didn't know if security was important in this area. Those bloody people in London never tell you anything.

Dust drifted across the roadside grass when I pulled up and cut the engine, The silence took over again. The white dust blew like steam across the grass. The roads here ran through chalk and there was a quarry gouged out of the hillside. The sun was past its zenith but I was still hoping I hadn't got here too late. The only real worry was that I didn't know what I was here for at all.

Even in the sun it was cold. I needed to move and the hill looked useful so I went up the road on foot, taking the binoculars.

From the top edge of the quarry all I could see were fields and farm buildings and the spire of the church in Westheim

7

some way off. Below the quarry was an abandoned plough rusting among brambles. There were no traffic and no one was working in the fields. There was nothing interesting to look at and I began feeling fed up.

All they had said was please station yourself in the area Westheim–Pfelberg–Nöhlmundt and observe. Only London could be so bloody vague.

Now I was stuck on top of a chalk quarry obediently observing an abandoned plough in some brambles at 12 times magnification. It would do London good if I trudged down there and took it to bits and did a one-tenth-scale sectional drawing and sent it in as *sighted* 1300 *hours map-ref.* 04–16 *Blake's Contour* 115-*A have no intention of reassembling*.

The fields were quiet except for the whisper.

Nothing moved anywhere. The farm buildings looked like cardboard cut-outs in the distance. Any traffic in this area would send up dust and there was no dust. Nothing moved on the land. The whisper was in the air. I looked upwards.

There was no vapour-trail and I had to do a square-search with the binoculars before I caught it. Small as a fly.

I looked down again. Dust was rising along the Westheim–Pfelberg road a couple of miles away near the spot where I'd talked to the farmer. No one could see me from there even on top of the quarry. It probably wouldn't matter if anyone did.

This had the smell of Parkis about it: move X into Square 4 and let him sweat it out, you never know your luck. After a dozen blind swipes Parkis would score a hit and people would call it a 'flair'. They forgot the times he missed.

The trail of dust was fading among the fields towards Pfelberg. Nothing else moved on the land. The whisper was still audible so I lay on my back and propped the binoculars up with my hands on my cheek-bones and adjusted the focus. The fly was very high now and vapour was forming. It was climbing to full ceiling in slow spirals and the sun flashed on it every time round. It was too small to identify but its performance was military and the only plane in the West German air-arm with this much ceiling was the Striker SK-6.

The vapour made a corkscrew in the sky. Most of my awareness was now shut in by the binoculars and I forgot the fields and the farm buildings and concentrated on the bright fly trapped in the lens. It spiralled hypnotically. The whisper was only just audible now. I put it at close on sixty thousand feet, the Striker's operational ceiling.

A new sound came in and I rolled on to one elbow and

searched for it. It was a heavy throb. Something red had started moving half a mile off, a farm tractor with a cloud of diesel gas forming above the vertical pipe. I watched it for a while and then lay back on the cold earth with the binoculars and located the plane again.

The vapour-trail had levelled off and there was a break in it. I saw or thought I saw that the machine's attitude was now horizontal. There was a lot of glare and I couldn't be certain.

I started thinking about Parkis again. The area Westheim–Pfelberg–Nöhlmundt was big, something like a hundred square miles, and inside the towns that marked it there was only agricultural land. Even one of Parkis's blind swipes wouldn't be aimed at information on red tractors or abandoned ploughs. On the other hand any information about an aeroplane observed at sixty thousand feet would be a bit thin, and you didn't have to come here to see a Striker SK-6. The Luftwaffe had five hundred of them in service and you could see a squadron airborne over various sections of the map on any given day.

The binoculars in my hands were vertical and the plane was dead-centre in the lens. Immediately over the area Parkis had briefed for me there was a military aircraft performing.

But Parkis couldn't have known.

The throb of the tractor went on and I wished it would stop because I wanted to listen to the sky and its silence. The whisper had gone now. The plane was still there, clinging to its ceiling with the jet throttled back, ten tons of potent machinery moving about directly above my head. The pilot was isolated, eleven miles from the nearest human being: myself. His isolation – and his contradictory closeness to me in the lens – appealed to me in an odd way.

Even with the peripheral light shut off by the binoculars the glare was strong because he was near the sun, so I leaned on my elbow again and rested my eyes on the green fields for a bit.

The tractor was dragging something heavy with a bright curved blade and the earth came up in a wave. Birds had drifted in and were foraging in the furrows. Farther away a truck was sending up dust along the Pfelberg–Nöhlmundt road. The air was dead calm: the dust settled where it had risen. The truck was audible now and I could hear the tailboard chains jumping. Above the sounds of the truck and the tractor another one was beginning. It was continuous and fine.

When I lay back and put the binoculars up, the plane flicked at once into the lens because it was bigger now. The vapour had stopped and the corkscrew motion was much tighter. The configuration was dart-like: the Striker SK-6 was a swing-wing and at that altitude the mainplanes would normally be in furled position twenty degrees from the fore-aft line of the fuselage and not showing much.

The sound was pitching higher and I could see the dark blobs of the air-intakes. The whole image was getting progressively bigger and now I could see the exact attitude: the plane was pointing downwards at a rotating angle near the vertical. I used the sun-flash to measure the rotation, counting aloud. One revolution per three seconds. The plane was in a 20 r.p.m. constant vertical spin.

The noise of the truck along the road had faded. The throb of the tractor was being gradually overlaid by the shrilling of the plane.

From the height where the dive had started it would have taken roughly sixty seconds for the sound to reach the ground: by that amount I was listening to the past; but as the dive went on the distance closed and sound was catching up on vision. It was now uncomfortable on the ear-drums. I couldn't estimate speed because the plane was almost head-on to the binoculars. In a vertical dive there wouldn't be any power on but the Striker was built to stand 1500 knots and it could reach that speed by gravity. All I knew was that this scream was the sound of something going very fast.

Time started telescoping now and I was worrying. The plane was big enough at this stage to see without the binoculars and I dropped them and cupped my hands to block out the glare and watch the thing coming on at the ground without any sign of pulling out or any sign of being *able* to pull out. The shrilling was so bad now that it was difficult to go on thinking rationally because the primitive brain was telling me to *get up and run somewhere safe* while the modern brain was working out a few figures: the plane was now below half its attainable ceiling and coming on at something like its peak attainable airspeed which put it at a mile for every four seconds and that gave me fifteen seconds to get out and there was nowhere to go.

Then the whole sky went dark as the plane's shadow passed over me and the noise was so loud that I was on my feet and running by the time it hit the ground a hundred yards away. The impact was explosive and comparable to a medium-charge conventional bomb detonating just below ground level in soft conditions. Earth began falling on me soon after the shock-wave had passed and there was a spherical cloud of chalk billowing round the crater the plane had made. I was running into it and

10

through it until the fore-brain took over and stopped me. There was no need to run any more.

Then I began moving through the weird white light, lurching against my own shadow that the sun was throwing against the chalk. I could have believed I wasn't alone. It took a minute to reach the edge of the cloud and I was choking a bit. Mixed with the damp-cellar smell of the chalk was the sharpness of molten metal and kerosene. The flame-wave followed me and I had to start running again until I was clear.

The wailing sound got on my nerves and I had to stop and identify it: the birds following the tractor had flown to a group of elms and were still calling in fright at the explosion. The man had left his tractor and was lumbering towards the cloud of burning kerosene as if there were something he could do.

I found the binoculars and went back to the car, turning it towards Westheim. On the way there I realized something. Parkis *had* known.

Most of the post office staff were still outside and people were telling them what had made the noise, but one man was behind the counter and I gave him the number and hung about for ten minutes until the connection was made. London would get it by the overt intelligence sources in a few hours but they wanted it quicker than that or they wouldn't have sent me here as an observer. They hadn't warned me to use speech-code when reporting so I compromised and just said: 'The fly fell down.'

Chapter Two

BRIEFING

People with Pekingese grow to look like Pekingese.

The Bureau doesn't officially exist, so everyone there has grown to look anonymous. They are flesh and blood but you never quite know whose flesh or whose blood they consist of today: you get the odd feeling that during the night there was enacted an unspeakable rite involving flesh-eating and blood-letting by some refined form of extrasensory transference and that the A-positive you were talking to yesterday is now Rhesus-negative.

The permanent staff at the Bureau have another thing in common. Whenever I show up there they look as if someone has left a dead rat on their desk. They looked like that when I flew in from

11

West Germany and asked to see Parkis. It took nearly an hour to get into his room: he is very high in the Whitehall 9 Echelon and his room is behind what amounts to a series of distorting mirrors constructed on the principle of the Chinese Box, the idea being that halfway through the system you give up and ask for the street.

But I wanted to see Parkis about the fly so I kicked up a bit of fuss and they finally got the message and sent me into his room. This is the room with the smell of polish and the Lowry. It's a good picture but it has associations for me. I was standing under this picture the day Parkis invited Swanner to resign. Swanner had mucked up a mission and three of us were present when Parkis stood there with his hands clasped in front of him and his small feet together and broke the man up while we listened. We didn't like it. Parkis should have told us to get out first. I was standing under this picture the day when Lazlö put a pill in his mouth before we could get to him. That was all right: he was finished and knew it and did the sensible thing and at least he died in civilized surroundings instead of where they would have put him if we'd thrown him back over the frontier. But he was on the floor and already turning green when Parkis told us to 'take it away and get it buried'. We didn't like that either: it was said for effect.

The worst thing about Parkis is that he is the most anonymous-looking of all at the Bureau. His face is so ordinary that it could only be a mask and his eyes are like holes in it because they are colourless. He stands so still that you feel you could walk up to him and go on walking right through him and not notice anything but a slight chill on the skin. But you'd come out Rhesus-negative.

I was standing under the picture now. It's the only place to stand, because of the disposition of the desk and the filing cabinets and the briefing table. It may be arranged like that because when Parkis talks to you he looks at the picture most of the time, just above your head, to remind you that you don't exist any more than he does, any more than the Bureau does.

He had got up when I came in. He stood in front of me with his hands clasped together, looking at the Lowry.

'How was Munich?'

'All right.'

They'd pulled me out of Munich to watch the fly.

'Did anything happen there?'

'Munich?'

'Yes.'

'I sent in my report.'

'Ah.' It sounded as if he hadn't seen it but I knew he had. They would have pulled me out before long anyway for lack of 'positive lead-in data', by which they mean the smell of anything fishy.

'I expect you'll be going to Paris, will you?'

'No one mentioned leave,' I said.

'Waring is due back.' He looked at me instead of the picture.

'There was nothing doing in Munich. That was as good as leave.'

'Not quite Paris, is it?'

'This aeroplane,' I said.

'It isn't for you.'

'Why not?'

'You're a shadow executive.'

He turned away.

'Why was I sent there?'

'To observe.'

'Well I did.'

'But you didn't observe anything. It just fell down, so you said. We wanted to know why.' He was staring out of the window at the winter sky.

The portfolio on his desk had a word on the cover.

'That's all I saw. You read my report. It just came down like a ton of bricks.'

The word on the cover was *Striker*.

'Quite.'

'Look, is it because I mucked up the Bangkok thing?'

'I don't think you mucked it up, did you?' He turned round again and I could watch his face, the mask with the colourless holes. 'We're giving this one to Waring.'

'Why him? He doesn't know anything about aeroplanes. He doesn't know which end the flint goes in.'

Parkis stood very still. 'It's not really about aeroplanes.'

I was getting fed up. 'You send me out to a precise map reference just in time to fetch a Striker SK-6 on top of my head and now you say it's nothing to do with aeroplanes.'

The thing that nettled me was that I wanted to know something and I couldn't ask him. He'd sent me to observe a Striker crash that he'd *known* was going to happen, even to the time and the place. I wanted to ask him how he'd known.

'Not really,' he said.

I tried an oblique level. 'You wanted confirmation.'

'We have to put someone on it.'

'Waring.'

13

'Yes.'

'Why him?' Nobody likes Waring because he can't work without a closed-circuit transmitting system and a bullet-proof jock-strap: he's got a 'low threshold of psychological stress', which is Bureau terminology for being shit-scared.

'Because he's due back from leave and sufficiently refreshed.'

'I've never been fitter.'

He looked down from the Lowry. 'Why are you so upset, Quiller?'

'I want the mission.'

'Yes, I can see that. Why?'

'I was there.'

'Ah.' He waited, and I knew I'd have to give him more than that.

But it was personal. The fly in the lens. His loneliness up there eleven miles away from the nearest human being: myself. The silence in the sky and then the long scream and the crater and the shadow I'd lurched against in the weird white light of the chalk-cloud. Personal.

'And I'm interested,' I said, 'in aeroplanes.'

'Ah.'

I wanted to hit him. Everyone does.

'Look, is it something I could be good at?'

'Something . . .?'

'The mission. Is it my cup of tea?'

He turned slightly and stared at the wall-clock. 'It isn't really a question of that. It's a question of time. I've already assigned a director.'

'That doesn't affect me. I can start getting my clearance straight away, then he can brief me.'

'We might have to change him.'

'Why?'

'You might not want to work with him.'

'Who is it?'

'Ferris.'

'I'll work with Ferris.'

He looked at the clock again. 'It's an overseas area.'

'You can jump me in.'

He smiled. It was the fixed smile of a ventriloquist's doll. 'You really want this one, don't you?'

I knew then that I'd sold it to him. It hadn't been difficult. Later I knew why it hadn't been difficult.

*

14

There was a flap on when I went through the departments for clearance and it took longer than usual because everyone was under pressure. I went through Accounts, Codes and Ciphers, Credentials, Firearms, Field-briefing and Travel. Accounts made me go through the motions of examining my last will and testament – did I want to make any changes? There was nothing to change: the wording had stood like this for years *Nothing of value, no dependents, next-of-kin unknown*'.

When I left the building there was one of the Federal Republic Embassy cars outside but it might not have been anything to do with the flap.

They drove me to the airport alone and I didn't see Ferris until I was weighing in. We didn't say anything before we got on to the plane.

Ferris was a thin man with hollow cheeks and horn-rimmed glasses and the remains of some straw-coloured hair that blew about when he walked. He looked like a clever young electronics engineer on the verge of a nervous breakdown, except for his steady eyes.

'How much did Parkis tell you?'

The power was easing off and we slipped our belts.

'Nothing much. Someone tipped them off that another SK-6 was due to hit the deck and I was sent there to confirm.' I watched the lamps of London dimming away below.

'Have you had anything to eat?'

'No.'

'Eat while I talk.'

The girl was wedging the trays in and we helped her. The seats behind and in front of us were empty; a woman with two small children was across the aisle. I knew Ferris had checked this; he was good on security. When I began on the mutton he said:

'You'll know some of this because it's in the papers. West Germany's got five hundred Devon Aviation Striker SK-6 swing-wing aircraft in service with the Luftwaffe as part of NATO's nuclear and conventional air force. It's a good machine, adaptable, versatile, got a flexible performance although it's sophisticated, and it can cope with reconnaissance, interception, ground support and bombing. The German Defence Ministry's cost estimates were too optimistic and the development outlay escalated the production bill to six hundred million pounds sterling, but it's a firstclass strike plane and everyone was happy with it until it started falling out of the sky. In the last twelve months they've lost thirty-six of them in high-impact crashes and the pilots can't tell them what happened because they're dead. The pattern's always the same as the one you saw.'

I wondered where Ferris had been when I was on top of the chalk quarry. 'When were you called in?'

'They had to brief me before I could brief you.'

That was all I'd get as an answer. I'd worked with him before and he only told you what he thought you needed to know.

'I had to persuade Parkis,' I said.

'Did you?'

'It wasn't difficult.'

'How's the chop?'

So I shut up and he said: 'Nobody's at all happy now. Devon Aviation are bothered and they've sent out some of their people to work with the Accident Investigation Branch of the Ministry. They've had a permanent A.I.B. team of wreckage-analysts over there since the tenth pattern crash. They've got bits at Farnborough and they've rebuilt most of one Striker from a few thousand fragments. The aviation physiologists are trying to be busy but they haven't got much to work on – you saw that crash so you can imagine what the pilot looks like afterwards. So far no one's turned anything up. Everyone's miserable. West Germany's worried because it's their plane and the U.K.'s worried because we built it and NATO's worried because the Luftwaffe squadrons are part of their striking-force. You want some more of that?' He edged his dish of French beans on to my tray. He'd let the girl give him a tray in case I needed seconds.

'When do I eat next?'

'It depends how busy you get.'

'What's a "pattern" crash?'

'The ones that go straight in, like the one you saw. They've been getting normal accidents as well – control-locking, power-failure, bird-strikes – but they've only lost four planes and one pilot from those. Without the pattern crashes the SK-6 would have a comfortably low accident rate. Of course they've had a few cases of the pilot baling out in a muck-sweat from sheer panic. The Striker's a rogue aircraft and they've only got to notice the clock's a minute slow and they're hitting the ejection tit.'

'Are these things crashing anywhere else?'

'Not on that scale. The U.K. and French accident rates are normal-low.'

'It's particular to Germany.'

'That's why they say someone must be getting at the planes.'

It was Peach Melba again. I took his as well.

'Why are we interested?'

'We're not.'

He was trying to be cagey again so I said: 'Then what the bloody hell are we doing in this aeroplane?'

'We're not interested in helping Devon Aviation or the Luftwaffe or NATO. It only happens to be Strikers crashing: it could be cruisers sinking or reactors blowing up.'

This agreed with what Parkis had told me: 'It's not really about aeroplanes.'

I said: 'We're interested in why somebody's trying systematically to knock out a cold-war weapon.'

'Why,' Ferris said, 'and who.'

'That's not all.'

'All for the moment.'

I sulked for a bit and he didn't break the silence. I don't like being used as a hooded falcon. I couldn't do anything about it, of course. You're cleared, briefed and sent in, and if you ask any questions outside the prescribed limits of the briefing they think you're nosey or windy and they're usually right. The man in the field isn't given the overall picture because there are always background factors that might worry him if he knew what they were. It works all right but on the other hand we always go into a mission knowing there's an awful lot going on in the background on any level from the Foreign Office to the hot-line and we tend to worry about it because we don't know what it is.

When the girl came for the trays I pulled out the stuff they'd given me in Credentials. My name was Martin and I was an aviation psychologist attached to the A.I.B. team operating at the Luftwaffe base at Linsdorf where two of the pattern crashes had happened. I assumed they'd picked on Martin because it could be either English or German according to which I wanted to be at any given time. There was nothing special in this lot and it looked a bit thin on the face of it but that might be because I'd pushed them into dropping Waring at the last minute.

Ferris saw me looking at the papers.

'How's your German?'

'West Hartlepool accent.' I said to show him I was still narked at not being told anything.

'You shouldn't need much cover.'

Perhaps that was why it looked a bit thin.

'Where do I start?'

'The thing is, there are two ways of going at the Striker problem.

You can analyse the bodies and the wrecks to find how the planes or the pilots are being got at. That's what everyone's already doing at Linsdorf and other places and they've not turned anything up. Or you can jump the queue and try to find who's getting at them and why.'

'You've said that.'

'Now I know you were listening.'

In half an hour the pressure came off our haunches and we began the run-in to Amsterdam.

It was blowing a half-gale and as we came broadside on I could feel the mainplane lifting on the starboard side. Dust from the freight area stung our faces and a hat took off and a man ran after it. We had to hang about for an hour before they called us for the Hanover flight and Ferris wasn't hungry and I'd just had a meal and neither of us talked because he wasn't going to and I wasn't going to try to make him. He wandered round and round the souvenir stall peering through the glass at the varnished clogs and packets of Clan, his thin straw-coloured hair blowing to and fro as he moved.

I'd stopped sulking now. Ferris was all right. I'd done two missions with him and he hadn't let me down. Now we were at it again: he was here to guide me, show me the way in and set me running like a ferret down a hole. Later he'd support me, feed me information and get my reports to London through the protected communications net; he'd pull me out of trouble if I was worth it or he'd abandon me and throw me to the dogs if I got in too deep and couldn't get out and looked like being a danger to them; then he'd call in a replacement and there'd be someone else eating his Peach Melbas for him while he told them as much as he thought they needed to know. It wouldn't be Waring. If I stopped anything nasty they'd never get Waring into the same area.

'Why do they have to varnish the bloody things?'

'To make them shiny.'

'But they don't look nice, shiny.'

'They don't know that.'

It was after midnight when we touched down in Hanover.

The normal routine would be to take separate taxis to different hotels and he still didn't say anything until we were through Customs and I thought he was leaving it very late this time.

'Start by seeing Lovett.'

'Where?'

'The Carlsberg.'

18

'All right.'

Outside at the taxi-rank he said: 'Did you pick anything up in Firearms?'

'Only the pox.'

Chapter Three

SELBSTMORD

There was no wind in Hanover. It was cold.

From the outside the hotel looked like a cinema organ designed by Steinberg. Inside it was an ornate cave full of lamps and shadows. It was quiet even for one in the morning, though people were about.

'But of course it isn't your fault.'

There were some piles of baggage near the main doors and more people were coming out of the lift, hardly any of them talking.

I said I didn't want to see the room. Number 14. Lovett was 31 in the register.

'It's just that my wife is sensitive about things like that.'

The American was consoling the manager and then consoling his wife, looking around secretively as if for a bar where he could console himself.

'If you will follow the page, Herr Martin.'

The other people were coming silently across from the lift.

'We don't have to stay, honey, but that doesn't mean it's their fault now, does it? We have to be fair.'

When my bag was in Room 14 and the page had gone I went up two floors and walked along the passage. It didn't seem worth waking Lovett if he'd already gone to bed. There was a light from under his door but there were voices from inside so I went down again because we would have to talk alone.

A piece of grit had got lodged under my top lid when we were crossing from the plane at Amsterdam and I spent some time poking about with the corner of my handkershief and thinking about Lovett.

It was a name from the past and I hadn't seen him for more than a year. He used to be with the Liaison Group and I'd worked three times under his direction, then they sent him to Rome on the Carosio thing and one of the adverse party found him alone and

19

left him for dead. It finished him for operations and the Bureau put him into their political section to sit in on summits and report any rot. He could still move about without crutches or things like that but he was full of platinum tubing and bone-rivets and his face was attractively lopsided so he never went short of a bed.

There was a NATO conference going on in Hanover this month and I suppose the Bureau had sent him to sit in on it.

It was a bit of metal, which explained why it had got lodged in so efficiently. The room looked watery now.

That sort of job must be irksome for a man like Lovett because he'd been very active before and spent most of his leaves in the Box of Squibs showing people how to break a door down without any noise and things like that: the Box is the house in Norfolk where we're sent at intervals for refresher training. But Lovett was good in subtler ways and perhaps he now passed the time trying to get two frames of micro under one full-stop without any tweezers.

I had to blank my mind consciously before I could get to sleep because I was still narked with Ferris for not telling me anything. Lovett would have to make up for that in the morning.

'He can't be!'

She laughed at first, like some people do, but her eyes were beginning to go bright and she went on staring at me with the laugh still on her face.

It seemed genuine.

I said: 'He threw himself out of a window on the fourth floor. Last night, about eleven o'clock.'

It was genuine all right. I got to her before she could hit her head on anything. She didn't go right under. When I helped her into the chair she stayed there without moving, like a dress thrown across it, but her eyes opened and she began staring again and I said:

'Have you got any brandy?'

After a minute she asked me: 'How do you know?'

'They told me at the hotel. I was going to talk to him this morning and that's what they said happened.'

There wasn't anything but beer and a dreg or two of vodka in the bottom of a bottle so I gave her that, but she didn't drink it. Her colour was coming back and she sounded almost normal when she spoke again.

'So that was Bill.'

She wasn't dismissing him. She just didn't feel like consoling herself with the usual deceptions: but there must be a mistake, I was only talking to him yesterday, so forth. She was the kind of woman who would appeal to Lovett. His wife would have approved.

'It's the official version,' I said, 'anyway.'

'So you know him well.'

'He wasn't the type.'

'No. What's this?'

'Drink it.'

'What do you think I am?'

It was a small room with a bunk bed and there were two dressing-gowns behind the door. I didn't know who the other girl was. They'd given me this one's name at the hotel. She was on the translating staff for the conference. I'd asked them who came to see him most at the Carlsberg and she'd been the only woman on the list and I thought she'd probably know him better than the others.

Ferris hadn't actually told me to start enquiring. It was the only thing to do.

He'd sounded upset. 'Well, they were on to it bloody early.'

'Did they see us coming through?'

'No. They don't know us.'

I listened to his breathing on the line. He was trying to think what to do now. He'd have to tell me a bit more, because Lovett couldn't.

'They must have got on to him a few days ago. You can't rig that kind of thing at short notice.' I could hear him sweating it out. 'That Striker you saw.'

'Yes?'

'It was Lovett who told us it would happen. You were sent out there to confirm. They must have caught his signal, something like that.'

Suddenly I got a glimpse of the background behind the mission, just a glimpse. Lovett hadn't been active since Rome. He'd been passing on information and it had been correct: the thing had come down almost on my head. Someone had told Lovett that the next Striker would crash at noon on the 29th in the Westheim–Pfelberg–Nöhlmundt area. Whoever could tell Lovett a thing like that must be someone who knew the whole works.

I'd been sent here to find him and Lovett was meant to tell me where to look. But they didn't want him to. They pushed him out of the window so that he couldn't.

'Is this thing off, then?' I asked Ferris.

'They've blocked our run.'

That wasn't the same thing at all. 'What do you want me to do?'

There was another pause while we listened for bugs. It seemed all right.

'Get in their way.'

The room seemed to go cold around me. You always have that feeling, a sort of goose-flesh that doesn't show on the skin. But I liked him for handing it to me without a tray underneath. Someone else – like Loman or Bryant – would have said well I don't really like to ask you and of course you know you can refuse, so forth. Ferris had just said go and bloody well do it. Get in their way.

Nobody likes it.

You can be told: they're holed up in that arsenal over there and you'll have to go through the barbed wire and round the machine-gun post and across the minefield and past the armed guard with the Alsatians, after that it's easy. And most of us will go in. It's not pleasant but we know what the odds are. However bad we know what they are. We're frightened but it's a different kind of fear, a more supportable one, from the fear of what we call 'getting in their way'. Because then we don't *know* anything. We don't know who they are or how many or where they are or what they're doing or why. We have to find them by letting them find us first, and they can be anywhere in a street or a lift or a car or a shadow and when we get close to them we might not even know it, might have our back to them. We always find them in the end. Always. But quite often the only thing we know about them is that they were the people who fired the shot and didn't miss.

'All right,' I told Ferris.

Before he rang off he said: 'You didn't actually see him?'

'No.'

They said he'd gone through a glass roof first and woken everyone up.

'You might put his stuff together and check it for anything useful.'

There wasn't anything useful. A picture of Sheila, some notes on the conference (they would be props), two tickets for the Operhaus dated tomorrow night, money, cigarettes, keys, the litter we leave behind. But I stayed a good hour in his room pretending to go through it and then asked the manager and the staff a lot of questions and then went back to his room and moved past the window quite a lot. Then I put his personal stuff together and posted it.

The only attention I attracted was from the police who wanted to know who I was. Someone in the hotel had obviously rung them up. They were perfectly satisfied that it was a case of *Selbstmord* because my unfortunate friend had left a note. I didn't advise them to compare the handwriting: perhaps it had been done on Lovett's portable and anyway they'd have used his own pen for the signature.

Then I went to see Sheila, the girl in the photograph, because that was what they'd expect me to do, call on his friends and contacts. No one tagged me when I left the Carlsberg.

'I suppose you can't give me anything to go on?'

She got up and tried to pour the vodka back into the bottle but her hand was shaking too much.

'What like?' she asked tonelessly.

'Did you see him with anyone? Was he alone when you left him last night? Did he talk to you about anything?'

She came up to me with dulled eyes and her voice on the edge of the breakdown she was going to have as soon as I left. 'I can't help you. I don't know who you are. Bill's dead. That's all I know. It doesn't matter to me how it happened. It might later but it doesn't now. I've got enough to be going on with.'

It hadn't been nice telling her the way I did but I'd wanted to know if she was involved. Pretty girls on the translation staffs at international conferences get a lot of attention from recruiting officers and some of them do things just for the kick.

I went to the door where the two dressing-gowns hung.

'When will you be seeing your friend?'

'My friend?'

'The girl you share with.'

'I don't need anyone.'

It began the moment I shut the door after me and I didn't envy whoever it was that the Bureau would send along to see his wife because that was going to be even worse. We ought not to marry or if we marry we ought not to do the things we do.

No one tagged me from the block where she had her flat.

During the afternoon I showed up a few times at the Carlsberg where the manager was looking more cheerful: apparently the exodus of guests had stopped. He gave me the names of a couple of people known to be friends of Herr Lovett and I went to see them but it was no go: instead of telling me anything useful they just kept asking me why 'poor old Bill' should ever have 'done such a thing'.

One of them was at the conference hall and I hired a car to get

23

there because it's easier tagging a car than a man on foot and I wanted to make it easy for them. It was a 250 SE and I chose the new grey because most of them were that colour and I didn't want them to think I was actually advertising or they'd wonder why.

I was still drawing blank by nightfall. Either they weren't interested or they thought that with Lovett neutralized the rot had been stopped. All I could do was hang about at the hotel. Normal routine in the case of a bump is to stay clear but sometimes we're told to go in and find out what happened, and quite often the people who did it will keep in the area hoping for more trade. This time they didn't seem ambitious.

Finally I got fed up and drove down to Wernerstrasse and had a meal at the Bavarian place on the corner and when I came out they were sitting in a dark-coloured Opel parked twenty yards or so behind the 250 SE. It was the one that had been outside the Carlsberg when I'd started off from there.

The thing to do now was to make them lose me without my losing them. It's not an easy operation but it's always worth trying because if you're lucky you can find out where they go and that's halfway to finding out who they are. Ferris wanted to know that and it would be nice to ring him up and tell him.

I got in and had a look in the mirror. There were some traffic lights a hundred yards behind where the Opel was parked and that was almost the ideal distance. They were red at the moment. One or two cars were going past, turning out from a street not far up from the restaurant, but it was better to wait for the main bunch of traffic that was held up at the lights.

When they flicked to green I started the engine and sat watching for a bit to judge the conditions. The bunch of cars were coming up from behind me, two abreast and stringing out. I decided to call this one a dry run and wait for the next sequence of lights: it would give the oil more time to get round the engine before I used it as hard as I was going to. The 250 SE had a shoulder-type seat-belt so I put it on, watching the mirror. The lights were at red again and the tail-end of the bunch came past and left the street empty on this side.

It would be useful to edge the revs up a couple of hundred while I was waiting but they might notice the gas-haze and it wasn't worth risking; the engine was at fair working temperature and there shouldn't be any flat-spot even under full gun. There was nothing coming up from in front of me on the other side. In the mirror the lights were green and I touched the gearshift into low and kept the clutch down. The only thing that worried me now was that it was beginning to look too easy.

They must have got their own engine running by now but that wouldn't help them: what they would need was a tank.

In the mirror the two leading cars were halfway down the empty stretch and closing on me fast from behind and it looked about right so I brought the revs up and the wheel hard round and put the 250 broadside-on to the bunched traffic in a turn so tight that I felt the nearside front stub-axle hit the buffer even though the weight was shifting aft under the acceleration. The initial wheel-spin cost a little traction but the curve was under control and I cleared the two leading cars with enough to spare although of course they didn't like finding me broadside-on across their bows without any warning and they were braking hard and hitting their horns as I straightened out of the U-turn and dragged at the gear-shift and headed for the lights with the power still piling on.

There was some noise behind me on the left as the bunch began shunting and breaking their rearlights but it wasn't my fault because continental drivers never leave enough room for their brakes and they're always leaving red glass on the roadway even when there isn't a 250 across their bows. But the noise wasn't serious so I knew that the Opel hadn't even tried. In any case they wouldn't have stood a chance of making the same U-turn after me because the first two cars had already passed them when I'd pulled out and they could only have rammed into the rest of the bunch and they didn't have a tank.

The start I had on them now wasn't much more than sixty seconds but it was the most these particular conditions could allow: the whole operation was controlled by the traffic lights and their time sequence and when they went red again the hundred-yard stretch would become empty and the Opel would have room to manoeuvre. The lights would have stopped my run and brought the sixty seconds' start to a grinding halt if it weren't for the side-street halfway between the lights and the restaurant, the one where a few cars had been turning out while I was waiting for the off.

I went into it just as the Opel got under way with a lot of tyre-squeal and came up the street in my direction. I didn't lift my foot to give them time to see me because it wasn't necessary: they knew I wouldn't head straight on for the lights – which were now red again – and there was nowhere else to go except into the side-street.

It took seven or eight minutes to lose them. It would have taken less than that to lose them entirely but I wasn't trying to do that: I had to stay near enough to find them again. There was a dodgy bit where someone had double-parked a yolk-yellow Volkswagen and I thought for a minute I was going to clip it but it was all right. The only risk was a one-way street which I had to take in the wrong direction but the single car I met there tucked in so fast to let me through that they must have thought they were going in the wrong direction instead of me.

The engine was smelling a shade hot by now because the acceleration needs had kept me in second gear all the time but the oracle had been worked quite nicely and I put her into third and slowed down for cruising as soon as we were back in the Werner-strasse.

They were the third car ahead and I stayed where I was for the moment. They seemed to have lost a lot of their excitement but they wouldn't be giving up until they'd combed the area in the hope that I'd pulled into a good place to play possum. They were doing that now.

One of the cars between us peeled off into the Bahnhof and I slowed to let a bus go past. There was more traffic about because people were coming away from the restaurants and the early shows and this was a help. The bus was a hazard though and when it drew in at the next stop there was nothing to do but overtake and expose the image of the 250 SE.

The Opel wasn't ahead any more. It was nearly alongside and we were in a group at some lights. I didn't turn my head to look at them but I knew they were looking at me. They must have spotted me some way back and they'd known I'd have to over-take the bus before long so they'd slowed under its cover and waited till I had to come past.

I decided to call the whole thing off for the night. They knew what I'd been trying to do: flush and follow. They wouldn't let me do it again so I wasn't going to find where their boss was and ring up Ferris and tell him. All I could do now was to get clear and hole up in a different hotel: if I went back to the Carlsberg the people at the Bureau would have to get out the form and deal with it, the one that said next-of-kin unknown.

The lights went green and I found a gap and took it and fouled into the wrong lane and got away with it and started a series of feints through the streets at the back of the Bahnhof but this time they were breaking all the rules too and the Opel left the mirror only twice before it came back again and sat there weaving about on its springs.

Then I lost them in a full turn at a roundabout and gunned up and found a right-angle and went in fast with the mirror still clear but there was only one lamp in the street and when I flicked the heads on there was just time to hit the brakes. It was a *cul-de-sac* and the 250 finished up slewed sideways within a foot of a notice that said if I parked my *Wagen* there the *Polizei* would be informed immediately. I hoped they would hurry.

By the sound of things the Opel was overshooting and braking hard and backing up. My lights were out by now but the *cul-de-sac* grew bright suddenly and I turned my head and saw the passenger-side door of the Opel swing open as it pulled up.

They turned off their engine and it was very quiet except for their footsteps.

Chapter Four

THE DUMP

There was a blank wall at the end of the *cul-de-sac* and they'd left their headlights on to see with, so that their shadows were very big on the wall. They came side by side.

They didn't rush. They thought I might have a gun on me. They came slowly and once or twice halted, ready to drop flat and fire from the ground. It looked a bit silly.

I sat where I was.

One idea would be to drop the gear into reverse and scatter them and try reaching the main street with the head well down and the fingers crossed. It was chancy because you can't dodge about when you're driving a car; you can only dodge the car about; they know where you are: stuck with the controls; and they only have to stand there and pump the stuff into you. No go.

The other ideas were worse so I sat there and worked up some anger about what they'd done to Lovett; anger is a prerequisite for action: it turns on the adrenalin.

I left my hands on the wheel for two reasons: I didn't want the indignity of having to put them there by order; and I wanted them there anyway so that they were free to do things quickly.

One of the men had fan-teeth which you normally associate with honest people of cheerful disposition but I didn't think this one was very honest and he didn't look cheerful. The other one smelt vaguely of almonds. They were both about my weight and I left my hands on the wheel while they frisked me and then one of them stood back a bit to keep me covered while his friend looked in the glove-pocket and under the seats and the dashboard.

They spoke with a Lüneburger accent.

'Where is your gun?'

'Please?'

'Where is your gun?'

'More slow of talking, please. I do not – '

'You speak better German than that,' he said and his friend laughed.

'Everyone has their off days,' I said. The laugh came again and I didn't like it. Perhaps it was the walls making an echo that distorted it or something but this man's laugh was a kind of wet guttural spasm as if someone was being carefully strangled. He was the one who smelt of almonds.

'Don't you have a gun?'

'No.'

'Why not?'

'The bang frightens me.'

Their faces were pale in the headlights. They both had hats on to look respectable. One of them wasn't happy about it and went diving about in the back of the car and I thought he must be taking the stuffing out of the seats. He was the kind who couldn't understand anyone not carrying a gun, which meant he depended on his own quite a lot, so he was the one I'd go for if a chance came.

'There isn't a gun anywhere,' he said.

'It doesn't matter,' his friend said.

They both climbed into the back of the car and shut the doors.

'What are you doing in Hanover?'

'Having a look round.'

'Who are you?'

'A bad-tempered ferret.'

'*Don't move!*' It was jabbed into my neck.

'I was going to show you my papers.'

'We're not interested in false papers.'

'Then I'll leave them where they are.'

'Yes.'

There was a rustling noise.

'Would you like some marzipan?'

I angled my head round politely. He was holding a packet to me with the silver paper half peeled off.

'Not just now, thank you.'

'Don't you like it?'

He was the one who couldn't understand anyone not carrying a gun either.

28

'Not very much. It's got prussic acid in it.'

'It's got what?'

'Bitter almonds. Not very much, of course. What you might call a homeopathic dose, but somehow the idea puts me off.'

They wanted me alive or they could have done it by now and left the body here: it was an excellent place and no one would come up here until the morning. They wanted me to tell them things first. They couldn't make me do that here because there's no really useful technique available when the subject isn't tethered: hurt him too hard and he'll get violent and it's no good waving a gun at him when he realizes he's got a value; you're not going to kill him with it because then he can't talk and he knows that.

'I like it, anyway,' he said. He began smelling of almonds again.

His friend with the fan-teeth said: 'We're not going to kill you.'

'That's good.'

'But after we've finished with you I must warn you to leave Germany. You mustn't think about it any more. He did himself in like a lot of people do, so why do you have to worry about it? Do you know how many people in Germany commit suicide?'

'A lot of people, you said.'

They were enjoying themselves and it worried me. It meant they'd enjoy 'finishing' with me too and sometimes that kind of situation can get out of hand: they go on for the pleasure and then it's suddenly too late; the sigmoid colon becomes too bruised or the blood-loss increases to the point where the heart starts trying to pump a vacuum.

'Yes,' he said. 'Approximately ten thousand every year. That's almost one every hour. So you mustn't think any more about him. Start your engine and drive back into the main road.'

They were very cautious, not wanting to do it here. It was an excellent place but they obviously knew of a better one.

I said: 'You've left your car in the way.' I looked round and through the rear window.

'Can't you get past?'

'I don't think so, but I'll try.'

'No, I'll go and move it. I've got to switch off the lights anyhow.'

He got out and his friend sat very still with the Walther P38 lined up with the bridge of my nose. The catch was off and his hand was dead steady. He'd stopped munching on the marzipan so that he could concentrate. His face was plump and the stare had a slight smile in it as if he wanted me to know that for him it was a special thing, to kill a man, a special pleasure, a substitute for orgasm, and that he wanted badly to do it and he would in fact do it if I made him and that he hoped I would make him.

I wondered who his controllers were.

'Switch your headlights on,' he said.

Just as, a little while ago, the time sequence of the traffic lights had governed that situation, unseen people – his controllers – now governed this one. Their orders, through the media of his memory and his motor-nerves, were operating the fixator muscles of his finger so that it remained still, three milimetres from the end of the primary spring's travel, two millimetres from the end of the secondary spring's travel and the percussion.

I would have liked to know who his controllers were. He had respect for them but I couldn't rely on that. All I had to do was make too sudden a move and the flexor muscles would contract in nervous sympathy.

'You want to do it,' I said, 'don't you?'

'Yes.' The smile was going out of his stare. 'Switch your headlights on.'

I thought I'd better do that. Target attraction is a fairly common phenomenon in most physical disciplines and if I let him go on staring at the bridge of my nose long enough he might easily lose his control.

It happens to military pilots on exercise, especially with dive-bombers: they home in on the target with such concentration that sometimes they become hypnotized and can't pull out. I wondered if the Strikers were always on dummy-gunning trips when they went straight in: but someone would have thought of that already.

His friend moved the Opel and doused the lights and we were sitting in reflected glare from the wall now that my own were on.

We listened to his footsteps coming back. If there had been a chance it was over now. The advantage had been that they didn't expect me to try anything while he was busy with the Opel. They both had faith in the gun even though there was only one of them with me. The main disadvantage had been the springs of the driving-seat: it would have needed an inflexible base for the body so that sudden movement wouldn't be shock-absorbed, giving the equivalent of a pulled punch.

'Good,' the man behind me said.

I knew he'd been watching me in the mirror but I didn't know he was so skilled: he understood that however poker-faced I was, the decision to move fast and suddenly would have shown in

30

my eyes a tenth-second before the muscles were given the order; and in that tenth-second he would have tightened his finger.

'You're jumpy,' I said. 'You need more sugar.'

'I do what I can,' he said, and bit off another piece of marzipan. His friend climbed in and said: 'Drive carefully.'

I put off the headlights and backed into the main street.

'Ernst-August-Platz.'

'Where's that?'

'Go left just here.'

Halfway along Georgstrasse the one with fan-teeth said:

'Switch off your headlights.'

'I did.'

'Yes, but then you switched them on again.'

'That was silly of me.'

'Yes.'

They'd seen people flashing me. I'd been hoping a patrol-car would decide to pull me up about it and ask to see my papers.

'Make for Südstadt now.'

The only other chance before we got there was when we were held up at some lights at the Stadtbibliothek. A policeman was hanging around. The exercise was easy enough: clip the wing of the car alongside and cause a jam and bring him across to deal with me. But I didn't trust them: they were pure German and therefore law-respecting but they or their group had finished Lovett and they might finish me with one in the spine and get out and run clear before a policeman could reach his holster. They might even chance a running duel in the street: the police sometimes open fire on running men and the papers usually call them 'gangsters' but now and then they're not gangsters at all; they're men caught in a bad spot somewhere between a high-level attempt to sabotage a summit meeting and the mechanics of the opposition lined-up against the idea. Men like these.

'Turn right in the square.'

We began heading for one of the main industrial sections. There were some lights on in the Sprengel chocolate factory and the three-quarter moon silvered the parapets and sparked on the glass.

One of them spoke quietly and the wet guttural laugh came again.

'Through the gates just here.'

I had to put the heads on. There were no lamps anywhere and the shadows flickered across the piled wreckage as we turned. They were stacked six-high: Volkswagen, Mercedes, Opel, Taunus, patches of rust-red and smoke-black, smashed glass and twisted axles and burst panelling. They'd been craned into orderly blocks with alleys between them.

'Stop.'

I put out the lights as if by habit because if there was anything to be done I wanted to start accommodating visually as soon as I could.

'Stay where you are.'

They got out and I sat waiting. I hadn't been brought here to talk, to be made to talk. It wasn't a rendezvous with anyone else. They must have meant what they said: I was to be beaten up and left incapacitated. In the flat light of the moon the wreckage looked like blocks of sculpting, monuments to the dead and the injured. The glass of a headlamp caught the light, an ever-burning flame. Did they assume I didn't know anything worth talking about, worth being made to talk about? They were right. The mission was in its first stage and all I knew so far was that it was a long drop from the fourth floor of the Carlsberg and that there was a girl in Hanover with too much pride to drink any vodka. The alleys between the blocks of wreckage were quite wide, the width of a mobile crane, and a running man would have to zig-zag like a forest hare: it wasn't much better than open ground. Whereas Lovett had known a lot: he'd even known there was one due to come down in the Westheim–Pfelberg–Nöhlmundt area and they'd had to make him forget.

The shadow of a hat was across the windscreen, a respectable trilby. They were standing still and listening to make sure no one would hear anything when they did it.

The shadow moved, sliding across the glass.

'You can get out of the car now.'

A little ball of silver paper flashed away and bounced.

He had a black rubber cosh in his hand, which I was expecting because it is the perfect instrument for paralysing the main joints with very little effort. The other one was standing back with the Walther P38 trained on the driving-door. It was a cold night and we'd been travelling with the windows shut and the smell of almonds inside the car was sickly.

'Come along, now. Get out.'

Apart from the special tactics they show you at the Box of Squibs in Norfolk there are the routine exercises that most people know. The handbook is written in Basic Civil-Service and this chapter is headed: *Taking Leave of a Stationary Vehicle While Under Menace of Fire-Arms*. But the actual idea is sensible and can work if you're very quick so I leaned over and hit the handles of both doors at the same time and jack-knifed with my feet against the driving-door and kicked so hard that the door's inertia helped to send me backwards and out through the other side before it swung against them explosively and put them off their guard for several fractions of a second. Some people say you should leave the door shut while you go pitching out of the other one so that it makes a bullet-shield and there's a lot of point in that but for one thing they can shoot through the window and for another thing the Norfolk Instructions are based on psychological rather than physical factors and the chief of these is the use of surprise.

They'd expected me to emerge past a slowly opened door and in fact I was moving hard in the opposite direction and the door was bursting open against the hinge-stop with a lot of noise and up to a point it worked because the first two shots went into the seats and the third rang somewhere among the wreckage in front of me as I hunched over and started the zig-zag with my hands hitting out at the stuff on each side of the alley to help the momentum while the fourth hooked at my coat and the fifth smashed some glass near my head. He was playing it the best way, keeping still and taking steady aim instead of coming after me and firing wild. Another thing that worried me was that they had a gun each and it was no good counting on the basic limitations of the P38: it's a 9-mm Luger with eight shots and so far he'd only used five but there was a near-synchronized double report now as the other one started up.

They were anxious by this time because I could hear them following but the moonlight was a help to me and a hazard to them: I wasn't doing anything that called for precision. All they'd done so far was to put one into the flesh, upper forearm. My left hand was sticky but only through hitting at the wreckage which had a lot of torn metal among it. I saw a blob on the ground and scooped it backwards and heard it smash against metal – it was a headlamp from one of the wrecks and it hadn't caught anyone in the face but it might have and you've got to try *everything* because people who get into a mortal situation and don't try *everything* are selling themselves short and that's what a lot of them die of.

One was closer to me than the other. It would be the one with fan-teeth. He was thinner. He was running faster. Barbed wire, a sweep of headlights somewhere on the other side, a lamp as high as the moon: they were all I knew. And his pelting footsteps behind. I span at right-angles along the edge of the dump, along the barbed wire, trapped in the hare-track of the dump and the wire, my shadow flickering beside me, thrown by the tall lamp, beside me and slightly ahead of me across the sculpted façade of the wrecks, then he fired again and the bullet struck and droned on, deflected and struck again and rattled among the black metal carcasses where I ran.

An irrelevant consideration (human pride) was trying to get my attention, make me stop and swing round and go at them, but it was dangerous and the instincts knew it and went on pushing me forward. You don't need Norfolk Instructions to tell you: never run *into* a gun.

Only one of them now. The thin one. His friend had stopped. He would be waiting somewhere at the other side of the dump to pick me off with a close calculated shot as soon as I came into range. It was no good going down there. The tall lamp swung as I turned again, then the instincts took over completely.

Their reasoning was sound: it was a geometrical certainty that if I stayed in the maze of the wrecks I would catch a bullet in the spine or the face sooner or later, a second from now or a minute from now. The thin one wasn't firing as often as he should be: he had become a beater and he was trying to flush me straight into the other one's gun. He would do that, would be bound to do it, as long as I went on running.

Headlights swept the wire again and I saw that it was close-rigged: four or five strands with six-inch gaps. The posts were angle-iron cut sharp at the top so I put one hand on the wire itself as near as I could to a post and went over the top with a shoe fouling and the wire dipping till I let go and dropped and tried to run and couldn't; my coat was caught by more than one barb and wrenching was no good and somewhere on the edge of the vision-field I noticed the flash as he fired again and came running on but you can get a coat off quickly if a lot depends on it and I was running again, running hard, my feet on the flat surface of tarmac.

The headlights were blinding but not too close. It was a vacuum horn, the kind that big trucks have. The tyres began dragging.

Perhaps the thin one followed because he had only two shots left in the magazine or because my coat across the wire made it easy for him. But he must have been frightened, to take no heed at all. The orders were to beat me up, to kill me only if I gave trouble. There would be nothing in the orders to countenance my getting free. So he must have been frightened of them, the controllers, to do so desperate a thing.

Or it was simple misjudgement. I knew there was time and I was clear across the road and lurching among frosted mole-hills when the big horn boomed again. Then there was the other sound, of something soft being hit, and I slowed my run, relaxing.

Chapter Five

THE WIDOWMAKER

It looked ugly on the ground.

Ferris had called it adaptable, versatile, flexible, sophisticated. On the ground it looked humped, bow-legged, sinister, obscene. Sexual.

Down here at Linsdorf they called it the Widowmaker.

I had telephoned Ferris.

The sun was directly behind it, a flat orange disc two diameters high in the mist. It squatted there, black. Why sexual? I had to think about it.

Ferris had ordered me down here to Linsdorf. Herr W. Martin Aviation psychologist attached to the Ministry's Accidents Investigation Branch. Walter: another name that could be English or German, whichever was the more convenient at any given time.

Because the wings drooped. They were held spread open and drooped like the wings of a crow in the act of copulation. That was why.

They were running the engine up. The kerosene haze darkened the sun, dirtied it.

The pilot was walking across from the crew's quarters, clumsy in his boots and anti-g suit, his oxygen helmet dangling.

Ferris had ordered me to Linsdorf for his own reasons. I didn't ask what they were. He was my director in the field.

'I told you you should have picked something up in Firearms.'

'I didn't need anything.'

'What happened?'

'We finished up playing "Last Across" and he cut it too fine.'

'You could have avoided a situation like that if you'd had a – '

'Oh for God's sake what do I want to shoot at them for? We want to send them to Parkis alive, don't we, so he can watch them do what Lazlö did after he'd bled them. Don't we?'

The black haze smothered the sun's disc, fouling it. There wasn't much sound: the acoustic irradiation was spreading away from where I stood. Only half-visible, only half-audible, the plane existed and didn't exist. You could believe you imagined it, that it was something out of a hangover, a black tumour on the sun.

'You don't have to be upset,' Ferris had said.

'That's good.'

I'd started out on a routine flush-and-follow exercise. Objective: find where they were based or who their contacts were and then signal Ferris like a good boy. I'd finished up without an overcoat and out of breath like a bloody fool. Of course there was no need to be upset.

He wasn't too jolly himself. If I'd stopped one in the lung all he could have done was signal London and try to wipe up the mess.

'You'd better get down to Linsdorf.'

I asked him to tell the car-hire people to keep their shirt on till the police found an abandoned 250 SE. That was what he was for, that kind of thing.

The pilot stood watching the plane, then suddenly turned round and trotted back to the crews' quarters and I thought: Surely he's not got the wind up already.

After I'd talked to Ferris I went round to Avis and picked up another one for the drive down to Linsdorf: a good-looking N.S.U. RO-80, the one with the rotary engine. I couldn't resist it because it was an engine I'd never tried. London Accounts would put up a bleat: *The type of motor-vehicle selected for routine transport in Hanover, West Germany, 1 November, appears excessively expensive in view of the fact that no Special-Uses form was filed in retrospect.*

The half-noise of the half-thing that stood there against the sun was dying away and I saw the silhouetted head of the flight mechanic prodding out of the cockpit looking for the pilot.

Signal to London Accounts: *Reference your observation concerning the hire of* 1 *N.S.U. RO-80 in Hanover I would respectfully suggest you go and stuff your cucumber up the Old Kent Road.*

Then the pilot came trotting across from the crews' quarters again, calling something to one of the ground staff. The flight mechanic climbed down from the plane and the pilot checked his report sheet and nodded and swung up and the mechanic passed him his helmet. The sun was clear now and beginning to dazzle.

Of course you can pick up a 260 k.p.h. Lamborghini and file a Special-Uses application in retrospect on the grounds that you'd had to chase someone in a Concorde before it got airborne. They'll believe anything: all they understand are the mechanics of parsimony.

The chocks were away and the thing was turning. It looked even worse broadside on with the wings flexing to every bump in the ground. I'd only seen them in the air before, once through the binoculars over Westheim and once at Farnborough Air Show eleven months ago: there'd been three of them and they'd looked pretty enough with the R.A.F. roundels and polished-metal finish and everyone cheering like mad. That was before they'd started dropping out of the sky all over Germany.

The N.S.U. wasn't the only thing. I couldn't go back for my stuff at the Carlsberg or they'd have made sure of me with a distance-shot so I'd bought the bare necessities at a supermarket on the edge of Am Kröpcke – toothbrush, shaving-gear, so forth – but I'd gone to town on the overcoat: it was a sheepskin job and a perfect fit except where the bandage was, right upper fore-arm. High collar and full lapels and extra length, right down over the bum and beautifully warm. It was a pleasure to stand here inside it watching that bloody aeroplane. *The type of overcoat selected for winter wear in Hanover, West Germany* . . . Cucumbers.

He was rolling faster and turning towards the end of the runway with the wings rising and falling and the recognition lamps winking, easier to see now because the sun wasn't behind him any more, then he was gunning up on tower permission and rolling again with the wings lifting and holding and the power piling on and the wake of dark gas streaming behind and then he was airborne so fast that the legs were folding before he came abreast of where I stood on the perimeter road already craning my neck. The sound hit me with a kind of protracted slam and indicated better than anything else that a mass of ten tons was being pulled upwards at forty-five degrees through an element that wouldn't support a feather.

He made one circuit and was lost within nine seconds. The airbase couldn't have been in his track because there was no sonic boom as I walked round the perimeter to the main buildings. The sky was totally silent.

They were stowing the chocks in the bay.

'Why did the pilot run back?'

'Who are you?'

'Martin, British A.I.B. group.'

'Have you shown your papers to Security?'

'I couldn't be here if I hadn't.'

'You must ask the Herr-Direktor of Operations.'

I went on towards the hangars. There was a pilot pumping up nis bicycle outside the crews' quarters.

'It was a nice take-off.'

'What?'

'I was watching his take-off. Very neat.' I didn't know their slang: it wouldn't be in any dictionary. The correct use of slang is like an accepted accent and can open doors that are shut to printed credentials.

He laughed briefly, undoing the pump and stowing the extension. 'Oh, they go *up* all right.' He was older than a boy and younger than a man, notably handsome, careful in his movements and speech. The strain marking this face would show on all of them: it was part of their identity.

'Did he forget something?'

'Who?'

'The chap who's just taken off.'

He clipped the pump back and looked at me uncertainly. 'What like? I'm sorry – I don't seem to be quite with you.'

'The pilot ran back for something. I was worried.'

He laughed again. 'We're all worried. No, he'd only forgotten his sea-horse. He often does that.'

The Striker was in the circuit again, much higher, much wider. We heard it faintly.

'I suppose he won't fly without it.'

'Never.'

He was wondering who I was. I asked him:

'What do you use, yourself?'

'Women.' The laugh was the same: part-nervous, part-cynical. 'I don't take them up with me but they're quite a tranquillizer.'

What would they dig out of the mess of alloy and blood and fibreglass and bone in the crater at Westheim: St Christopher, a rabbit's foot?

'My name's Martin.'

'Röhmhild.' His feet came together. 'Are you English?'

'Yes. Aviation psychologist.'

'Another one?' He corrected himself quickly. 'Maybe you're the one we've been waiting for.'

It looked as if a ton of grey lump-sugar had been tipped across the hangar floor in the chance shape of an aeroplane.

There were only six people working on it. The place was enormous, a tin cathedral, and cold. The heaters were on and it was less cold than outside by a few degrees. The cost of the heaters would probably have kept the whole squadron airborne for a week. The winter sun was up but it was brighter inside the hangar: lamps hung in focussed clusters from the gantries, their glare emphasizing the silence. Despite the movement of six men there was a mortuary stillness here.

'You know anything about orchids?'

One of the small doors at the side of the hangar came open and I looked across to see who it was. The survivor, the one with the wet guttural laugh, might be sent down here to look for me. I'd come to Hanover to see Lovett and Lovett had known when the

38

next one would crash so they might think it natural for me to move out to Linsdorf and take it from there. So I wanted to know who people were when they came towards me.

'Not much,' I said.

This was Philpott, leading the A.I.B. group. I'd been here for an hour and all he liked talking about was orchids.

The man who had come into the hangar was carrying a transverse coupling and he dropped it on to the thick-topped butcher's bench. It set up a pure vibration that echoed from the roof.

'Sound as a bell.'

None of the others came near. Pure vibration wasn't news. They were waiting for something that made a sulky clunk when you dropped it.

'I'm working on a tropical epiphyte called *Orchis Ledulum* at the moment. Grafting, you know.'

He was a short hesitant-moving man in a white dust-coat. He looked gloomily across the plane-shaped litter of metal and saw nothing to interest him there. But his reputation was big even at Farnborough and I supposed he was like a conductor at rehearsal, dozing off until a false note came, then he would hit the roof.

The man who had come in was tying a mauve label to the transverse coupling.

'What did you do to your hand, then?' Philpott asked me.

'Tin-opener.'

'Ah.'

A man with DEVON AVIATION on his dust-coat came over from the engine area. The engine was a slug-shaped lump encrusted with white ash and there was nothing they could do with it: the kinetic energy created by a gas-turbine running at full pitch on impact will melt most of its alloys.

'Did Andy check this, Mr Philpott?'

It was some kind of control-toggle.

'Have a look at the list, then give it a flame-test. He'll be back tomorrow. Is the other one like that?'

'I've not freed it yet.'

'Go careful, then. Andy's got hopes there.'

I followed him past the nose section. It was just a melted lump but he seemed pleased with it.

'Titanium. They know how to take it on the nose, don't they?' He gave a wintry smile.

'Would you expect to turn up manufacturing faults at this stage?'

'Normally. Not with the Striker. They introduced Zero Defects Programming at Devon before these things were built.' He gazed at me pensively. 'These Strikers are perfect when you roll them out. It wasn't like that a few years ago. You'd find anything left about inside, you could furnish a house with some of the stuff. Rivets, bulldog clips, hand-rags. A whole tablecloth, once. You know what we found inside a flexible tank a couple of years ago? Three-legged stool, milk a cow on it. Went down off the Azores with a crew of seven. Zero Defects is going to put a stop to all that. American idea. Rolls-Royce brought it into Britain. Why?'

'I just wanted to know.'

'*Design* faults are different. We can turn anything up.' He looked broodingly across the sea of fragments. By the time we've rebuilt this lot we can tell you how many kids the chief riveter's got and whether they're boys or girls. Of course it's getting more difficult for us these days. Look at that turbine. Now what can you do with that? The higher they go up the harder they come down. You imagine the noise this one made when it hit. Like a bomb.'

'I can imagine.'

The test-flame coughed into life across at the butcher's bench.

'We can turn up anything. Anything.'

'Have you given much thought to sabotage?'

'Quite a bit.' He was looking away from me, watching the colour of the flame when the component was passed through it. 'You've got to. Flags, frontiers, it's like a circus.'

When the flame went out I said: 'This isn't exactly in your department, but if the pilot loses control and hasn't switched to automatic what attitude does the Striker assume?'

'Nose-down at four or five degrees.'

We went across to the bench.

'It's negative, Mr Philpott.'

'Tell Andy.'

The man took a green label from the box.

'Then we could say, could we, that if they didn't want to leave any evidence they'd go for the engine?'

'Who?' There was a drip on his nose and he blew it, squinting at me above his handkerchief. 'Oh, I see. Yes. That's what they'd probably go for.'

He'd been drinking but he wasn't drunk.

'Psychologize me.'

A quick forced laugh.

'I'm off duty,' I said.

They held each other, both half-turned towards me, still moving to the music. The whole of her body was in her eyes as she looke

40

at me and I knew she would look at anyone like that, any man.

'Martin,' he said, 'wasn't it?'

'That's right.'

He said to her: 'Herr Martin.' He spoke to me without looking away from her. 'This is my wife.'

'Frau Röhmhild.'

'Nitri,' she said. The flash of her mouth took away some of the animal, brought back some of the child.

'Walter.'

'Franz. Franz, Nitri and Walter.' As if we had made some eternal pact. 'We will see you again.'

'Yes,' she said and looked back over her bare shoulder as I knew she always did, at anyone. They drifted away.

'She's charming.'

'Yes.'

His name was Eagner and he had a doctorate in psychology. We had met earlier and he was back in the corner again where I was holed up to watch people, especially the pilots.

Even for a peace-time officers' mess it was lush and the band had been brought in from Hanover. It was invitation night and the room was crowded: pilots and their wives and girls, admin. officers and attached civilian staff, the A.I.B. group and the Devon Aviation team. I'd seen even Philpott here brooding solitarily at the bar over his tropical epiphytes.

I looked at the door every time it opened. If they came at all they would come before morning: the moment their controllers knew where I was they'd send them in very fast so that I couldn't do them any more damage. I was more than ready for them because I hadn't cooled down much: a bandaged hand and a bandaged arm were all I'd got to show for last night's work and I badly wanted to signal Ferris with something good, something he could use, as a change from mucking it up.

And at the back of my mind I was trying to tell myself it wasn't true that Parkis had put it across me so smoothly that you could have spread it on toast. Because that was what he had done. I'd been through the situation twice and it stood up. Someone had told Lovett where and when the next Striker SK-6 was going to crash. Lovett had signalled London. Parkis had wanted it confirmed and he'd wanted it confirmed by the man in the field who was going to be given the mission so he'd sent me in from Munich to observe and report. I was already hooked when I'd gone to see him: he knew I was interested in aeroplanes and he knew if he could bring one down on my head I'd be more interested still.

41

But he was thorough: this one 'wasn't for me'; they were 'giving it to Waring'; there 'wasn't time' to change the director in the field if I didn't want to work with him. I'd have worked with Pontius Pilate and the Seven Dwarfs and he'd known that. I was a shadow executive and he'd made me sit up and beg for a sabotage investigation job and now I was doing it. I would have refused: he'd known that too. I'd tried to refuse the Berlin thing and after that Bangkok and he wasn't going to let me refuse this one.

The sole consolation was self-cancelling: Parkis wanted me on the Striker pitch because it might break me into something bigger before I was through and the odds against that were the same as the odds against any of his blind swipes: twelve to one.

There was one chance, one, of breaking into something bigger. Somewhere along the line I could turn up the missing link.

'. . . as well as I'd like to.'

He waved to someone going past.

'I see.'

The link. The man who had told Lovett.

'It's because my duties are rotational – I cover a dozen bases on a strict schedule and that doesn't give me too much time to meet with them, I mean as individuals.'

The man who had told Lovett could be in Moscow or East Berlin or Hanover or here in this room tonight but most probably he was dead because he'd been the primary leak and Lovett was only a contact and Lovett had gone through a glass roof and woken everyone up.

'You seem very popular,' I said.

But there was a chance.

'I fill a need. They need a father figure.'

He was speaking in English with an American accent. Most people in the Federal Republic who speak English do it with an American accent and sometimes you forget they're German and not American. In appearance he could have been anything: Austrian, Swiss, Scandinavian. He had light eyes and a strong nose and a habit of lifting his head when he looked at people as if he were fixing a sight on them, especially people in middle distance. He wasn't much taller than Philpott but he was more energetic, jerking his hands as he talked, swinging his head suddenly to note my reaction. He was doing that now.

I said: 'That's not surprising.'

'But what can I do? I send them for mud baths and psychoanalysis up at Garmisch-Partenkirchen. I talk to them before they take off and after they land. I give them sedatives and tranquillizers – quite often it's a sugar-pill and statistically they're almost thirty per cent as effective and that satisfies me because the speed of the nervous impulse is in the region of three hundred kilometres an hour and I don't like to slow it down even by a fraction.' His long thin hands were jerking again. 'You have to find a working balance between calming their minds and slowing their reactions, do you understand me? It is becoming very difficult here at Linsdorf because there hasn't been an accident for quite some while and they're waiting for it. Everyone is affected: ground staff, administration, their own families. Yesterday a request was sent out to the wives of all pilots asking them to refrain from telephoning for news whenever the squadron has just landed. Everyone is affected and I have my own private name for it: Striker psychosis.'

They had changed partners, Franz and Nitri.

'Is it better or worse at the other bases?'

'It is as you would expect. I have drawn graphs of the pattern. When I arrive at my next base I can tell at once if there has been an accident and how many days ago it took place. After two days the shock is absorbed and the anxiety dissipates quite automatically. The worst has happened – do you understand me? – and everyone feels better. Here at Linsdorf it is different now. Look at them. They are so gay. But that is forced. It is frenetic.'

The floor was small and they came past often. They didn't look across at each other. It was as if they'd changed partners for life. I watched Franz Röhmhild because I would need one of them – one pilot – for study, and it might as well be him.

'He is not a difficult one.'

'Which one?'

'Röhmhild. The one you are watching. His outlet is in – shall I say – human company. His wife's. Others'. That is very good. But some are difficult. They come to me with spurious complaints: headaches, vision, chest-pains. Of course I send them to the Herr Doktor Reitermann: he is a physician and I am not. But they don't keep the appointment. They come to me in the hope that I shall suspend them from flying duties and finally that is what I do because their stress has reached its threshold and if I let them go up they will only bale out and report an engine failure. That has happened. It will happen again. I would be delighted: what do we lose? One plane. Six million dollars. Who cares? The pilot is safe. But I am not delighted because he is no better: he is worse. He now has guilt feelings added to his anxiety. He knows he is a sham and a coward. Then he is finished. We do not let him fly again.' His head had swung towards me and he was sighting along his nose. 'I think that comes in your own field, Herr Martin?'

One of them was getting drunk. It was the one who'd run back for his sea-horse. He was doing aerobatics with his hands and there were people round him, laughing loudly.

'My job is to save money for my government,' I said.

'Doc! Nitri wants to dance with you!' Franz was going past with a new girl. I couldn't tell if he wanted to break it up between Nitri and her partner; it just looked like a pleasantry.

'I am a responsible married man! I cannot dance with girls like Nitri, you realize that!'

It was noisier in here now and there was a lot of laughter and you could hear the undertone, the fear of tomorrow.

'I think you are attached to the engineers,' said Wagner with polite interest. 'But I cannot see how a psychologist can help them. How is that?'

'When a pilot sends in a false report to the wreckage analysis team they can spend months looking in the wrong places. My job is to question the pilot and find out if he's lying. Especially if he's reported engine trouble.' I kept my voice low so that he'd get bored with missing the odd word or two and let it go but he was listening hard.

'Engine trouble. Why?'

'It's the only bit of the plane we can't examine. It's just a lump of burnt-out alloys. And the pilots know that.'

'Yes, I understand.'

He was still watching me and I had a choice. I was on thin ice and I could either keep as clear as possible of Wagner or try to work with him. If I could work with him I'd learn more but he had a doctorate and there was the risk of blowing my cover. I chose the risk because it could pay off if I used great care.

'That's where you could help me. You know these boys better than I do.'

His head swung away. 'I would be delighted. You say you are trying to save your government's money. Is that modesty or cynisicm? What you are really trying to do is to discover the cause of the accidents and to prevent them. That will save many lives. It is my own ambition.' He was facing me again and saying forcefully: 'Herr Martin, I am averse to the waste of men like these. They are the youth and the future of Germany. I shall willingly sit in with you at a pilot's examination and shall invite you to attend my own. Co-operation can only – '

The one at the bar, the one who was drunk, had finished some aerobatics with his hand and now his hand drove downwards vertically and the stiffened fingers hit the teak surface of the bar and sent a glass crashing. The only sound after that was his laughter and when it stopped there was a hush in the room. People turned away from him.

A murmur came from Wagner. 'He should not have done that.'

'Let's hope he never will.'

Halfway into Hanover along the autobahn the rain came and I switched on the wipers.

'Either with her or someone else. He has a wide choice. Is that the phrase? A wide choice.'

She was curled up on the seat with her shoes off. Not very animal now, nearly all child. And hurt.

'It doesn't mean anything to him,' I said.

'Only at the time. It's the time I think of.' She stretched and pushed her fingers through her hair. 'But I have my times. I think of those too. It's wild, isn't it? Grotesque.'

Her speech wasn't slurred. She might have been cold sober: it was hard to tell. A lot of them had drunk steadily the whole evening, more than they normally did, more than they would be drinking now at some of the other bases – Spalt, Oldenburg – where the 'anxiety was dissipating automatically' after the accident.

I said, to make her talk: 'It's rough on everyone.'

'It's not like I suppose a war is like, when everyone's in it. They're on a sort of list. A waiting-list. Only just the few of them. Sometimes I think of him as already dead, and there's only the waiting for it to be official. That's when I forgive him most. Have you a cigarette?'

I checked the glove-pocket to see if there were a packet left behind.

'It doesn't matter. I don't want to smoke. It's cosy in here. What car is this?' The reflection of her hair was a cloud of silver on the windscreen and sometimes her nails flashed through it as she brushed it back.

'It's an N.S.U.'

'I don't drive. I lost my licence. I didn't even hurt anyone, only myself, but they took it away. It's grotesque.' We listened to the rain and the wipers for a long time. The lights of Hanover made a sudden haze on the horizon to the north and then vanished as we dropped again below hills. 'He wants to have as many as he can while there's time. All right, we can't live together any more but I'm his wife and we're in love, I think. But how much of what I feel is because I might not know him for long?'

I checked the mirror regularly and slowed a little when lights came. They all went by.

45

'He seems very confident,' I said. 'That's an important safety factor.'

'He's enormously brave. Fantastic record, almost as good as Otto's. He's come out of three crashes, I mean ordinary ones, not the special ones.' What Ferris called 'pattern crashes'.

'Were any of them due to pilot error?'

She swung her head and made a laughing sound though it wasn't quite laughter. 'You don't know Franz. He can bring in a plane backwards.' She was still watching me. 'He says you're a psychologist. It must be like undressing people.'

'It's much more difficult. You've got to get through a dozen overcoats before you can reach anyone's mind.'

'He says you're English. I'm wild about the English. You don't talk.'

'It's just that you can't hear, because of the overcoats.'

'There's the city,' she said. 'Where are you staying?'

'At Linsdorf.'

'But I thought you were going to Hanover.' She shifted sideways on the seat to face me, her legs still drawn up, one arm along the top of the facia. She was no closer to me than before and her scent was no different but suddenly she made herself explicit: her proximity, her scent, her body. 'You came specially?'

I said: 'Anyone would have given you a lift.' A lot of the cars I'd slowed for had been coming from the air-base after the party broke up.

'I know. But I didn't think you were coming specially.'

'What would you have done if you'd known?'

'Nothing.'

We drove through Hanover-Messe and up Hildesheimerstrasse. 'Let me know, will you?'

'I'm in Lister-Platz.' She looked for her shoes. 'Will you come in for a drink?'

'I don't think so.'

'Did you want to ask me about Franz and the others? To get information?'

'No.'

'Then we'll have a drink.'

The apartment was small and overheated and untidy, with her clothes around and nothing to show whether it was from indifference or despair.

She sat curled up on the floor just as she had been in the car, in the attitude of a child. The blatant carnality she had shown in the crowded room was quite gone, because the necessity had

46

gone; but her reasons remained and she spoke with her head turned away.

'It's late, and I don't want to have to go out again. If it can't be you it'll only have to be someone else.'

Chapter Six

NITRI

He looked dead.

There was no traffic about. It was late: gone 2.00 a.m. I had left the N.S.U. in the Hohenzollernstrasse and we'd walked round the corner into Lister-Platz. I had walked back along to the car and there was condensation inside the windows, otherwise I would have seen him from farther away.

He was only just recognizable through the condensation: some thin straw-coloured hair on a lolling head, black-framed glasses on a waxy face, the eyes shut. I looked along the street, both ways, both sides, in the doorways, in the shadows. It could be a booby-trap, you can never tell. They hadn't got on to me since the truck had hit the thin one but they were looking for me, I knew that.

The street seemed all right. I wasn't expecting a shot: it would be a rush of feet. They were controlled by someone circumspect. Even when they did a bump there was a suicide note to smooth things over. I knew now why they'd taken me to the car dump. They knew that if I gave trouble they'd have to shoot and they didn't want to do any shooting in the *cul-de-sac* with a lot of buildings around.

I walked once round the car. None of the doors had been forced. It looked all right so I got in and he woke up.

'I must have dozed off.'

'Don't let me disturb you.' I was a bit annoyed: not with him but with her. She'd thrown a few hysterics when I told her it wasn't on and hysterics can be wearing.

He was completely awake within seconds. 'I've been in signals with London all day. It goes roughly like this: Parkis didn't know a thing except that another Striker was going to crash, but he thought something much bigger was in the background – he's got a flair that way. That's why he wanted you for the mission. But there was nothing he could give you except what looked like a one-and-ninepenny sabotage-investigation pitch. So he had to hook you in.'

I began wiping some of the condensation off the glass because if anyone came by I wanted to see who they were.

'London got a letter today from Lovett, posted two days ago with a microdot inside.' He turned to look at me for the first time. 'They badly want to know who told Lovett about that Striker. They think it's someone trying hard to get across. He made contact with Lovett, who played it cool and asked for a sight of his wares. They weren't bad, were they? The exact prediction of the next pattern-crash. So Lovett was ready to pass him on but his signal about the Striker got intercepted. That was bad luck.'

He was silent for a bit and I didn't ask any questions. Even in an organization that doesn't exist and where everyone is anonymous there are some people whose names begin to mean something over the years. We'd all liked Lovett and I knew Ferris had worked close to him until they'd carved him up in Rome.

'We still want to know why the Strikers are going down. It's not the storm-centre but it's the way in, or one of the ways in. And we want to know, fully urgent, who made contact with Lovett.'

He must have actually been on one of the protected communications networks, person-to-person with Parkis. 'Storm-centre' was a typical Parkis phrase, straight out of the comics.

I said: 'What makes you think he's still alive?'

They'd neutralized Lovett just because he'd seen a fraction of the picture. His contact must be in possession of the whole.

'We think he's still in Hanover and the Bureau's monitoring the news of every death in the area. So far they believe he's not among them. Find him as soon as you can. Help him across. London wants him badly.'

'Oh come on, Ferris, you can do better than that.' I was suddenly fed up. Parkis didn't run all the missions but he was running this one and he was running it in his usual way: sparking off random activity in the field without a sign of co-ordination. 'They want me to find out why the Strikers are going down so my search-area's Linsdorf and they want me to find Lovett's contact so my search-area's Hanover. Tell Parkis to make up his bloody mind.'

'Nobody loves Parkis, do they?' He was running his long fingers across the facia-board, transferring his reactions. He spoke mildly for maximum effect. 'But you'll have to bear with him this time because he's on to a rather big show and you are in it. If you let your dislike of Parkis affect your judgement you'll come un-

48

stuck, and I don't want that to happen because I'm in it too and I'm responsible for you. So brighten up a little and we can do some good business together.' He ran his fingers round the chronometer and then took his hand away. 'Your judgement's a degree cloudy at the moment. Our contact tipped off Lovett about a Striker crash and the nearest Striker base from Hanover is Linsdorf so he might be there, someone on the admin. staff or on the technical side, even one of the engineers. And your enquiries have brought you back to Hanover tonight – correct? So you can commute between the two. Parkis doesn't realize that, but I do, and I'm not going to tell him he's got his wires crossed just because you're in a tantrum. Wouldn't she let you, or something?'

This was why Ferris was such a good director. He knew how to set you up when you were slipping.

'You really are a bastard,' I said.

'That's right.' He resettled his glasses. 'Another thing is, Parkis wants to send in a shield.'

I didn't say anything right away because I was feeling better now and in any case this was confirmation that the mission was expanding: they only send someone to look after you when things hot up and you become valuable to them. A shield is a bodyguard, close or remote, and his job is to stop people messing you about – people like the man with the marzipan – to keep you alive and leave you in peace while you're working. Some of us accept the idea because it can be useful: when Miller burst open the Warsaw thing last year it was almost wholly due to the shield who kept him alive while he was busy penetrating.

'No go,' I said.

'That's what I told him.'

'I work best alone, you know that.'

'That's what I told him.'

He'd been enjoying himself, telling Parkis the answers before I'd been given the questions.

'All I haven't told him,' he said carefully, 'is whether you've dug up any lead-in data at Linsdorf.'

'I've been down there for twelve hours, remember?'

'That's all right. I just asked. Because he will. How's the hand?'

'Top condition.'

'And what else was it? The arm, wasn't it?'

'I still don't want a shield.'

'Fair enough. But you'll have to be careful. Independence is one thing but as your director I'm not standing for any flights of bravado. Is there anything else before I go?'

I asked him for a statistics breakdown on the complete series

49

of pattern-crashes to date, chronological, geographical and with background information on the dead pilots. He said he could do it for me.

'Can I drop you off?'

'I'll walk. It's a fine night.'

I watched him away while the engine was warming. He had a loping stride and his thin hair blew around his head as he passed below the last lamp before the corner.

The Hanover–Kassel autobahn runs almost due north-south and I could see the few lamps of Hildesheim to the right. The rain had stopped and the three-quarter moon sent a trickle of light along the chrome edge of the screen. After Hildesheim I pushed the N.S.U. to its optimum cruising-speed on the auto-converter, close on 160 k.p.h. Full pelt was 180 but there was no need for that: the mirror was clear except when I overtook a night-running truck.

It had come oddly from someone like Ferris: 'You'll have to be careful.' Yesterday morning he'd told me to 'get in their way' without hesitation and now he was talking in terms of a shield. He'd known I wouldn't agree but if I'd changed my mind an hour ago he would have signalled London by now and they'd have flown one in. The thought was luxurious: once they decide you've got a value they'll do your buttons for you if you can't be bothered, give you that 260-k.p.h. Lamborghini without a Special Uses chit.

I missed her nyloned legs, curled up in the glow from the facia. Her scent was still in the car.

I'd stopped being annoyed with her because the stuff Ferris had given me was important and I was interested in it. It had been nothing more than frustration in any case because there'd been arousal and I hadn't bargained for that.

When I told her it wasn't on she slipped out of her dress, stretched, stooped and was naked before I had time to say that I meant it.

She was pleased, watching my expression, standing there with a little half-proud smile. 'I'm different, aren't I?'

Anders was the word. The lamp had a rose shade and she moved so that its light could play on her. Then I looked up at her eyes and she was sure of me and came towards me so I turned away and that was when the hysterics began.

I let them come. I couldn't leave her until I'd heard enough to know she wouldn't do anything *dumm* as soon as she was alone. They were all living on their nerves, the wives of Linsdorf, and if there were any dangerous instability in her a small shock to the ego like this could push her over the edge. Between sobs she said the expected: she hated me, I was impotent, so forth, throwing herself face down across the bed where the lamplight fell so that it was necessary to look somewhere else because for a lot of reasons it wasn't on and it was no good the libido's trying to struggle.

Then of course she was suddenly asking, 'Is it because I'm different?' and I went over and played with the hair at the nape of her neck because she was serious now and needed comfort.

'You're not that different, Nitri.' Her hair was like warm cream through my fingers. 'The English don't talk, remember? And there are other things they don't do when they don't want to, however, much they want to. You only want to hurt yourself and I'd make it worse, it'd be a kind of rape, wouldn't it?'

When she was quiet and I moved away and she watched me open the door. She said: 'You don't understand.'

'I'll tell him we did. That's all you want, for him to think so.' The Harz peaks on the left, moonlight along their snows.

He'd stayed in the mirror for more than five kilometres now so I came down to 140 and he still didn't pass and I began thinking things but he pulled out after a while and I kept my speed down until he became a shrinking blob of light far ahead of me. Some night-drivers like company through the long dark autobahns and he was just one of them.

The lamps of Nordheim. Poor little bitch. Not long out of school and into marriage with a man who used variety for a tranquillizer because his nerve was going and now she was only at peace when his plane took off because it was the one place where he couldn't take a woman, the one place where she didn't want him to be: alone with the Widowmaker.

But I would have to see her again. There was more that she could tell me. Ferris had asked if I'd dug up any lead-in data at Linsdorf. Well yes. But not entirely at Linsdorf: it linked with something she'd said in the car on the drive north. And she knew them better than anyone, the pilots, those who knew that she was *anders*.

There were a few lights in the motel and I swung the N.S.U. into the park and had a thought and turned out again without stopping, driving on for three kilometres and then taking the minor road past the airbase. It ran within a hundred yards of the hangars and they were on to me right away: red lights, mobile barriers, the full treatment.

'*Halt!*' One on each side with submachine-guns. '*Ihre Papiere bitte!*'

Their breath clouded in the lamplight. '*Von wo kommen Sie?*'

'Hannover.'
'Wo wollen Sie hin?'
'Nach Linsdorf ins Motel.'
'Was machen Sie auf dieser Strasse?'
'Ich muss wohl auf der verkehrten Strasse sein.'
'Lassen Sie den Wagen hier und begleiten Sie uns.'

I got out and they took up escort positions. The post was on the far side of the hangars and the guard commander kept me fifteen minutes and used the telephone twice before he was satisfied.

'Sie können gehen. Das nächste Mal bleiben Sie auf dem richtigen Weg.'

'Jawohl.'

Then they walked me all the way back and I still wouldn't fall into step and it got on their nerves. When I backed up and turned in the narrow road the headlights swung across the hangars and the statuary of armed figures.

I had needed to know. If anyone were getting at the Strikers it was from the inside.

You can use a book face down or a penknife on edge but I prefer keys and I always carry three on a ring and leave them in a top drawer because they'll go for the top one first and if someone interrupts they don't have time to open the lower ones.

I never vary the pattern: the rim of No 1 just touching the E of Yale and the rim of No 2 super-imposed on the border-moulding of No 3. They're no use to anyone, except to me. The only things they'll open are a '65 Chevvy in Mexico, a flat in Putney and a jemmied strong-box somewhere at the bottom of the Nile.

A book isn't so certain. They might not take it out and if they do they won't *necessarily* put it back face up. The snag with a penknife is that it won't *necessarily* fall over and if it does they'll smell a rat if they're any good at all. But they're certain to pick up keys: any keys. They'll try them on anything in the room and if they have the time and the equipment they'll make a wax impression. (I've used this set for four years now and there must be dozens of keys that can open the Chevvy and the flat and the strong-box.)

My room at the motel was like most others: you couldn't move the bed out of sight of the windows. In this case there was a balcony. The wardrobe was built in but I wouldn't have moved it to shield the bed anyway because they don't search your room and shoot afterwards: it isn't consistent.

It was soon after five o'clock when I turned in. Two cars left

52

the park in the few minutes before I slept, their lights fanning across the ceiling. The motel was on a route used a lot by commercial travellers. It might have been a couple of commercial travellers driving away.

Last waking thought: so they'd got on to me but there must have been a policy-switch and for the moment the orders were to leave me alive.

Chapter Seven

COLLAPSE

It happened at precisely 0951 hours: I checked my watch from habit.

'She is beautiful.' The manager nodded.

Most of them had gone, much earlier. I had slept until someone had called out across the park below my room: the human voice probes deeper into the sleep-levels than other sounds in the normal range.

I drank coffee at the bar. She stood on the lid of the black padded box. The traveller turned her to catch the light. The work was delicate: the mouth, ear-whorls, fingers.

'Original,' the manager said, 'of course?'

'Copies are a waste of time. A good copy can be valuable these days but people won't offer you a decent price, just because it's a copy.'

The paper was upside down from where I sat. There was still hope for the seventeen miners. Maria Fedrovna said she had not asked for asylum but that both she and her choreographer were 'considering such a step'.

The manager lifted the shepherdess to look at the markings on the base, his big hands gentle because he knew that if he dropped her the price would be double.

'Dresden, Herr Benedikt?'

'Of course.'

Feldmarschall Stöckener was killed late last night on the outskirts of Hamburg. He was alone in the car.

'Things are different there now. The bombing made a difference. My wife is there. My family.' He turned to me. 'Do you know Dresden?'

There was hope in his soft hooded eyes.

53

'It's some time since I was there.' The Wall and its extensions had gone up in 1961.

'Everything has changed now. Except my wife. My family.' He took the shepherdess and fitted her into the case among the others. I watched his face in the mirror behind the bar. He wasn't wearing a hat: it was on the table behind us with his gloves and this week's *Stern*. He had been wearing a hat before, crossing from the lift in the Carlsberg with the other people three nights ago when the American had said his wife was sensitive about things like that. I wasn't certain. Hats can make a critical difference. I would need to see him walk: people can turn their faces inside out but they never think to alter their walk.

His face was sad. Perhaps about Dresden. Or Lovett.

'How much is that one?' the manager asked.

'Do you want to buy it?'

'No, I just want to know how much a thing like that costs.'

'It would depend. I take them to a man in Kassel. Not a dealer. A private collector. He doesn't buy all of them. I'll be coming back this way, if you're still interested.'

'I'm not. I just wanted to know.'

'I would make a price for you of course. You talk to a lot of people here. That would help my business.'

The sound was dull, heavy and distant.

I looked at my watch. Benedikt hadn't heard, or didn't think it meant anything. Perhaps he thought it was another sonic boom: they were a part of life in Linsdorf. The manager had heard and was looking at the windows. He had lived here long enough to tell the difference.

I went outside and he followed me and we stood looking at the sky and listening. You can't hear a sonic boom without hearing the plane afterwards. The sky was silent.

'What was it?' he asked me.

'I don't know.'

I got the N.S.U. and drove straight there.

When I reached the main gates there was some traffic coming through: three or four official Luftwaffe cars and an ambulance and crash-party tender. They knew there'd be nothing for the ambulance to do but it had to be sent out for the look of the thing.

People were at the windows of the admin. buildings and groups stood outside just talking quietly. There was nothing to see but they'd come out because this was where the noise had been, outside, and it was the noise they were talking about. It had been like this in the streets of Westheim when I'd gone into the post office.

The A.I.B. team was standing in a group in front of the wreck-age-analysis hangar and I talked to Philpott. The rest kicked at pebbles, their arms folded, some of them looking at the sky. One of them said: 'They're gaining on us. We've not put this one together yet.'

'Did your friend find you?' Philpott asked.

'Yes.' Ferris would have telephoned the A.I.B. chief and Philpott had probably passed him on to the barman at the Officers' Mess. Good barmen knew everything and this one had seen me leaving with Nitri and he knew her address: she was an officer's wife. Ferris had gone there to hang about and when he'd seen me go into her flat with her he'd decided to wait. The most comfort-able place was the N.S.U. and any director can open a car without any keys: it's in the Norfolk Instructions.

Or it was one of several permutations. Ferris would have found me wherever I'd been; it was part of his job. I wondered if the noise had registered as far as Hanover: it was north of here and quite distant. There was nothing he could tell me to do about it that I wasn't here doing.

Some of the pilots were standing outside the crews' quarters and I walked slowly into the pocket of atmosphere that Dr Wagner had mentioned: I would have known there'd been a Striker down even if I hadn't heard it go in. It was the kind of atmosphere you can almost feel on your skin.

Franz Röhmhild was there with Artur Boldt and some others. Boldt was the *Geschwaderkommodore* and I'd talked to him last night: a lean slow-moving Rhinelander with no philosophy in his eyes. Most of the pilots accepted the situation: the Striker was a rogue aircraft and their orders were to fly it and as far as they were concerned it was a game of Russian roulette – I'd heard that phrase more than once at Linsdorf. But their *Geschwader-kommodore* had to lead them into the air and hope to bring them all back again and it affected his nerves differently: his natural fear was turned directly into anger against the top brass of the Luftwaffe who wouldn't ground the Striker until someone had found out what was bringing it down.

They weren't talking much. They stood looking at the sky because it was where they lived and where one of them had just died. A young *Oberleutnant* was trying to laugh it off:

'We're all right for another hundred days – who's complain-ing?' The pattern-crash average was one in ten days and there were ten main Striker bases operational. It was the Russian roulette attitude again.

An SK-6 straddled one of the dispersal bays not far off. In full daylight it looked as ugly as it had looked at dawn yesterday.

I asked Röhmhild who it was.

'Paul Dissen. You met him last night.'

The one with the sea-horse. The one who'd been doing aerobatics with his hands at the bar.

Dr Wagner came up and the atmosphere changed in a subtle way that I only just caught. Under the surface it seemed he was their god. Not quite. Redeemer? No: shepherd. Saviour. I had the impression that if Wagner were actually to fly with them on exercise they would believe they were totally safe.

'It should be the last one.' He addressed Boldt, perhaps because he was their *Geschwaderkommodore*. I'd wondered what exact line he'd take: he hadn't come across to the flying-crew quarters to pass the time of day. Their nerves showed in their eyes and their hands and their silence, and his job was to do what he could about it. 'This isn't a technical problem, you understand. The answer is available and the authorities may be obstinate but they are not blind.' His head was lifting and he looked at the others, sighting along his strong jutting nose. 'The generals blame the Defence Ministry and the Ministry has its face to save because it was responsible for ordering an aircraft that has proved itself dangerous. But there are pressures even at political level: the Americans inside NATO are urging Bonn to abandon the Striker's nuclear role and of course someone must eventually realize the absolute sense in that. Each time there's an accident these pressures are increased dramatically – that much is obvious, do you understand?' His light eyes surveyed them: he needed their reaction so that he could turn his argument and lead their attention into whatever channel would console them. 'So this could be the last one to happen before these planes are grounded. There has to be a last one and it will be soon.'

Boldt said quietly: 'It's not the plane.' He was looking across at the brutish shape on the tarmac. 'It's the pilot.'

Franz gave one of his short bitten-off laughs and the sound of it, the coldness in it, didn't help the others. He watched Boldt with his eyes flickering. Boldt said:

'I'm not talking about pilot *efficiency*.' His anger had been sparked off. 'You know that, Franz. You know it perfectly well. I mean pilot *condition*.'

Wagner was watching them both. He said to Boldt: 'You have a theory, I know. You've mentioned it to me.'

'Several.'

A telephone was ringing somewhere. I happened to be looking

56

at Franz and his shock was physical. The others turned their heads and turned away again.

I knew that Wagner would have tried making Boldt open up about his theories in case they were dangerous to morale: Boldt was their leader and his opinions counted. But no one would be able to speak until someone inside the crew quarters answered that telephone.

Even little Wagner couldn't do anything. The silence was total, of the kind in which background noises made no difference: a traffic-control vehicle was droning round the perimeter road but they didn't hear it. Vision was the only sense with any significance and so they looked at the ground, the sky, the humped shape of the Widowmaker.

The telephone had stopped ringing and after a minute a door was jerked open and someone called to us.

Paul Dissen was sitting in a corner of the reading-room like a trapped animal. He watched us as we came in.

Dr Wagner had given me the picture on our way here.

'The M.O. wanted him hospitalized at first but there's nothing wrong with him physically except for slight traumatic lesions in the face and corneae. I believe he would brood too much in a hospital bed because he is overburdened with guilt-feelings, and nursing attention – sympathy of any sort – would of course aggravate them. It is better he should be free to roam where he likes for today and talk to anyone who will listen. His psychological need is to be hurt a little and we should bear that in mind during the interrogation. Of course you *know* all this, Herr Martin, but I am just pointing out that his experience seen in the light of his personal background provides a typical case, which makes it easier for us – and for him.'

Dissen got up as we reached him and Wagner motioned him down. His eyes were bloodshot and some of the cheek-area capillaries had burst, leaving red patches like those on a painted doll's face. According to his report he had baled out at forty thousand feet, which would have exposed him to something like two hundred knots in free-fall before the chute slowed him to thirty through the upper layers.

We drew up a couple of chairs and Wagner said cheerfully:

'You've had an expensive day, Paul my good friend. Six million dollars. Never mind, we're delighted to see you back. I suppose you decided to panic, did you? Well, you're not the first.'

One had to get used to opposite-thinking. Dissen was a man in need but it wasn't the need for comfort. I remembered the faces of the pilots outside the crew quarters this morning when the door was jerked open – 'News of Paul! He's all right, he baled out!' There had been no spontaneous relief. One or two of them had looked deceived: the hundred days' grace had been denied them and it could happen tomorrow, a real one, a pattern-crash.

'No, *Herr Doktor*, I didn't panic.' He said it very deliberately. Wagner had triggered the reaction he was after: Dissen must be reminded that he had access to self-defence.

'You know Herr Martin, don't you?'

'Yes.'

'He's interested in what happened.'

Wagner had invited me to run the interrogation with himself sitting in. Dissen said to me:

'She began breaking up, that's all.' It was said with hostility.

'Do you know much about planes?'

'By "breaking-up" do you mean structurally? Structural failure?'

'That was what it sounded like.'

'Vibration? Fluttering?'

'Not quite. I'd call it resonance.'

'Nothing visual.'

'No.'

'Resonance. Has that happened before with the Striker?'

'No.'

'Not with your plane – I mean have you heard about it happening?'

'Sometimes.'

'So when it happened in your own plane did you remember having heard about it?'

'I didn't have time. I was too busy checking the display.'

It wasn't exactly a lie. He would have automatically checked his display as soon as the sound had come in. He would certainly have remembered hearing about resonance but fear would have driven the memory straight into his subconscious so that he could rationalize: *she's breaking up and I'm getting out*.

'Was the display in order?'

'The booster looked a bit unsteady.' He glanced with his suffused eyes from me to Wagner and back. 'You don't necessarily see anything wrong with the instruments when the whole plane's breaking up, surely you know that?'

Three pointers: 'looked a bit' didn't mean 'was'. And his glance to Wagner had been an appeal. And his defence had turned to attack: was I such a damned fool as not to 'know that'?

I didn't like doing this but I had to because Wagner was here and I could blow my cover if I dodged it. That could go a long way: Wagner had official influence and would get me thrown out of Linsdorf and it was part of the mission to stay here and ferret out all I could.

I tried him on limited channel capacity. 'Have you ever felt overloaded in the Striker? Failure to assimilate?'

'Sometimes. We all feel it sometimes.'

That would be true. The input signals and output demands of a sophisticated aircraft put a strain on the pilot and they were working on the problem everywhere.

We talked about environmental stress and he said he was happily married and 'didn't give a damn' about money. He spoke faster as we went on because he wasn't being made to talk about the plane. He hated the plane because it had exposed his weakness.

Wagner cut in to say Dissen's wife was 'quite charming, quite charming' and that she would be so relieved to 'have more of his company' from now on. Wagner had told me on our way here; 'He's finished, of course, as a pilot.'

I tried him on isolation stress: 'When the resonance began did you get any sudden feeling of loneliness? Did you feel cut off, lost in the sky, out of touch with help?'

'I had my radio. I reported what was happening.' His tone was hostile again: we were talking about the plane.

Wagner took over for ten minutes, keeping his approach cheerful, his hands moving energetically as he blamed the Striker, all the Strikers, going along with Dissen in his hate of them. Then I harked back to the technical aspect because it was meant to be my job and Wagner knew it.

'You must have been certain that the resonance would turn to actual vibration – fluttering or juddering – before long.'

'Why?'

'I mean if it was loud enough to start you thinking of baling out it must have sounded progressive. Critical.'

'You don't know what it was like.' He was standing up suddenly, his red eyes looking at neither of us, his hands jumping to his pockets and jumping out again to make defensive gestures. 'All right – I panicked. You expect me to stay in a plane that's breaking up under me?'

Wagner pushed his chair back.

'No. That's why we give you an ejection seat. You are expected to use it. And you did.'

I walked back with Wagner to his office.

'He will be okay now.' He had switched to American again. 'But I don't know about your "resonance".'

'All I can do is pass it on.'

'Otherwise it was satisfactory. We induced him to admit he panicked so now it's going to be easier for him. We had one of them shoot themselves, do you understand? Up at Bederkesa. The son of an upright Prussian family – he did what they expected of him, of course. But Paul won't do that. We didn't save the machine but we can save the man. I ask for no more.'

'They should all do that.'

He supervised our table personally, perhaps hoping to bring down the price of the shepherdess.

'You wouldn't have any Luftwaffe left,' I told him.

'Who wants the Luftwaffe? There's no war.' He spread his big hands. 'Let them take all the Strikers up nice and high and come down by parachute. Then they wouldn't get killed any more.'

The noise this morning had upset him.

Benedikt had been here when I came in from the air-base soon after dark and I asked him to eat with me because I wanted to know why he'd searched my room. He sat with his hands folded on the edge of the table, his soft hooded eyes sometimes looking at the other people. Neither of us faced the door from the parking area but we could both see it without turning round too far.

He had dropped the *Kasseler-Zeitung* on to an empty chair. It was the evening edition. 'They are toppling,' he said, 'in high places.'

It had been decided that Feldmarschall Stöckener must have got into a skid because there had been rain. His name was lower down the page, taking second-best to Hermann von Eckern, Minister of the Interior, last night relieved of his post following an incident in a Hamburg night-club, details of which were not yet revealed.

I wondered whether these two items were anything to do with the 'rather big show' that Ferris had talked about or whether Stöckener had just skidded and von Eckern had just taken a boy into the cloakroom.

But Benedikt seemed to think they were connected so I said: 'They'll be pushing them out of windows next.' I ordered liver and carrots because they both have something like four thousand international units of vitamin-A and I like seeing as much as possible in the dark.

'That poor fellow,' he said. 'What was his name?'

'I don't remember.'

He couldn't know I wasn't certain. It would be risky for him not to admit at once that he'd been at the Carlsberg.

'A lot of guests were upset. I left the same night, myself.'

I thought if he'd arranged to have Lovett pushed out of that window I would do something about it very soon. We don't often have a reason for doing a bump; it's usually just because the pressure's on. I said:

'Don't you think he skidded? Stöckener?'

A man and a woman came in and we looked round idly. 'I question why the chief of the Bundeswehr should be travelling alone in his car. Surely he would have a military driver.' He was eating very little. He wasn't a man for an appetite: sad-faced, withdrawn, cautious. Or perhaps he wasn't always like that. Perhaps it was his nerves. He might have told them: he's down here at Linsdorf and tonight would be a good opportunity. Because he wouldn't do it himself: he hadn't the build and it would have to be done quietly without too much fuss, which meant at least two operators.

'What about von Eckern?' I said.

It might be his nerves, not letting him eat. Because of the waiting.

'I also question why a *Bundesminister* should allow himself to become party to an "incident" of the kind that could lead to his dismissal. It doesn't seem very discreet.'

'Is everything to your satisfaction?' The manager was back, adjusting things on the table.

'Entirely,' Benedikt said, watching some people come in. The night was cold; they had pinched faces and rubbed their hands.

'Did you sell all of them, in Kassel?'

'No. I have some in my room. Are you still interested?'

'No. I just wondered.' He went away.

I supposed there *was* a chance that it didn't connect, just as there was a chance that Stöckener had simply got into a skid, but it would have to be tested out so I said:

'They don't fit anything, really.'

'I'm sorry?'

'The keys. I just leave them there so as to know if anyone's been poking about. What were you looking for?'

The pale lids rose and for the first time I saw his eyes fully and saw that he was frightened. I hadn't expected that and it threw me and then I understood. He said in a moment:

'We must be careful.'

He'd folded his hands again on the edge of the table to keep them still.

'You weren't very careful before. You got him killed.'

'Yes.' His voice broke on that one word. He could have said:

61

Indirectly. It would have been true: Lovett had known what he was doing and he should have taken more care but it was this man who had put him in hazard. Now he was doing it again to someone else. To me. I said:

'We'd better not waste any time.'

'There is no time. His face was grey and he looked tired suddenly and I knew that collapse was taking place. Inside Benedikt a whole edifice was coming down. All the things that had gone to the making of him as a child and a boy and a man, all the experience of half a lifetime that had brought him at last to a motel in a Weserbergland village to sit here with a stranger, all that had ever meant anything to him was coming down and soon it would be rubble. I didn't know why. I only knew that it was happening because in our trade we see a lot of it and we know the signs when they come into a man's face. They see quite suddenly that it's no go: they've come too far and can't find their way back or they've taken too much on and haven't the strength to see it through or they've started hurting too many people and they realize that their high-flying ideologies don't give them immunity to conscience when it comes to the crunch.

In a savage whisper he was saying: '*Get out of here.*'

Perhaps he hoped to save something of himself by saving me. I asked him:

'Who's doing it? Sending the Strikers down?'

'There's no time. *You must leave here.*'

He wouldn't even bloody well listen. I leaned over the table. 'Who is *doing* it?' I was getting fed up because while he was busy collapsing I wanted to snatch the odd brick out of the rubble before it was too late, 'Did you tell him? Lovett?' He was slowly shaking his head but I didn't think it was meant as an answer: he was shaking his head at the whole of life or at least the life he knew. 'Well you're going to tell *me*. What's their name?'

'*Die Zelle.*'

'Where's their base?'

No answer.

'Who's the top kick?'

He stared at me.

'*You have to get away.*'

'I'm busy.' He hadn't got the guts to give it to me straight, couldn't admit it, face the responsibility. Once they start collapsing the whole lot goes and they're irresponsible, treacherous, and the most you can do is try to shore them up and get some last desperate sense out of them before it's lost in the roaring of bricks. I said through my teeth: 'Who runs it?'

His face rocked and his eyes closed as if I'd physically hooked one on him and I knew how important it was that he should save my skin but I wasn't interested because it was his conscience he was trying to save and so far as it suited my book he could stew in it.

A man came in with a briefcase and Benedikt heard the door and opened his eyes and stared at me again because he daren't look round: he was using my face for a mirror. He was pretty far gone so I said: 'What've you got on paper? Memos, documents, anything useful? Any micro stuff? We can decode it, don't worry about that. Come on, Benedikt.'

The manager was at the far end of the food-bar staring at him and then staring at me. Benedikt looked ill and he was wondering why I wasn't doing anything about it. He started towards us and then thought better of it.

Benedikt was still watching my face.

'Who just came in?'

'One man. Only one.'

Of course I would have got him away before now and handed him over to Ferris. But I'd made a mistake and I didn't want to do it again. I'd been so aware that they would come for me again that I'd fallen for an assumption: anyone searching my room must be an adverse party. It wasn't until I'd seen the collapse setting in that I'd known who he was. That had been a mistake.

The next mistake I could make would be another assumption: that he was totally allied to me. You've got to mind your fingers when you give a dog a bone.

'Look,' I said. 'We'll accept you. You can be in London by tomorrow. But I've got to have something more definite first.' *Die Zelle.* The Cell. He could have invented it off-hand.

He wasn't listening.

The restaurant was half-full now and getting noisy. There were no curtains; the headlights of cars coming in made a kaleidoscope of the opaque sculpted glass of the windows. The espresso machine shrilled.

I looked at Benedikt. He sat like a sack.

'You can still make it,' I told him. I had to lean half across the table because of the noise.

But I could see I'd lost him now. It's something almost un-natural to witness: they just slip away as if they were drugged and you could time the process. Suddenly between one minute and the next they abandon interest in doing what they were recently desperate to do. (Ferris had said: *They think it's someone trying hard to get across.*)

Final throw.

'We'll go now. We might as well. We can talk later.'

Some kind of consciousness came back. He said:

'If it were as easy as *that* . . .'

Headlights froze across the glass and dimmed away.

'It'll get easier as we go along,' I told him. 'This is the roughest bit, that's all.'

Then they came in and I knew he was right and that it was too late.

Chapter Eight

THE PALLBEARERS

'Is he all right?'

'What did you say?'

It was very noisy.

'He looked ill. Is he all right?'

'Yes. But bad news.'

The beer was making them raucous. A lot of laughter.

'What sort?'

Headlights.

'His wife.'

'Tch! He talks always about his wife.'

Leaving. Not arriving. But no one had come through here.

'Are they lawyers?'

'Who?'

'The people who came to see him.'

'Friends. Just a couple of friends.'

Benedikt had got up and gone across to talk to them and they had stood there for a few minutes and there was no point in sitting somewhere else with my back to them because they knew I was here. Now they had gone up the stairs.

'That's bad, then, if it's his wife.'

'Yes.'

'He talks a lot about her.'

'I know.'

The staircase came halfway into the room and was very modern with glass at the sides, the same thick opaque glass that the windows were made of. He'd made an effort before getting up and some of his colour had come back. He had just given me the name of a place – the clockmaker's in Neueburg – and then he'd gone across to talk to them. I hadn't expected them to go up the staircase, all three of them, like that.

I picked up the *Kasseler-Zeitung* he'd dropped on to the chair and looked through it because they were making it so obvious. All I had to do was walk out and get into the car and drive away.

The manager had gone back to the food-bar.

Lyon had beaten Hamburg 3–1.

The farther away I got from them the less I'd like it. I preferred to keep in close because they wouldn't expect that. I waited another fifteen minutes and then went across to the staircase. A group of travellers stood at the bottom with tankards waving about as they talked. They'd had a good day and were pleased with it and wanted me to join them but I said I couldn't just now.

The corridor was all right: there were no recesses. But his room was towards the far end and that was unnerving. It meant full exposure in confined quarters for something in the region of fifteen seconds and there was sweat inside my hands when I reached the door. The light was on in the room but there were no voices.

I gave it a minute and tried the handle and pushed the door open and gave it another minute before I went in. A gust of laughter came up the staircase and I shut the door so that I could think better. The curtains were drawn and I left them like that. There was almost no point in looking around because I couldn't see any signs of hurry and unless they'd been in a hurry they would have done a thorough search, but you never know your luck and I saw to the furniture first. It didn't take long: most of it was built in and I wasn't checking for hollows or magnets because he didn't live here permanently.

There was only one valise and most of the stuff was dispersed in the room and I checked the shaver-case and squeezed all the tooth-paste into the wash-basin. The black box he kept the figurines in gave nothing. It had come open for some reason and the only two pieces that had been inside – a faun and a shepherdess – were smashed on the floor near one of his outstretched hands. It looked as if he'd been taking them out of the box when they did it.

There were hollow sections among the bits and I checked them: the head of the shepherdess and one half of the log she was sitting on, the hind quarters of the faun. But they were empty. Finally I searched the body: pockets, linings, heels, inside the watch, inside the lighter and the three pens, going through the full routine while the hooded eyes went on looking at the fragments.

As I stood up I wondered whether he might not have been happier, more fulfilled really, selling these things between Hanover and Kassel instead of trying to slip the skids under people who travelled in violence. I believed even at that stage that Benedikt had never been first-class agent material. Ideology isn't enough. It seems enough: it's blinding and belongs to the heart. But it won't save you from being found one fine day on the floor with a cheese-wire mark on the throat.

It had occurred to me to telephone Ferris.

The night wasn't much above freezing and I was glad of the sheepskin coat. My breath was grey in the sharp air as I stood looking about. Everything seemed all right. If in point of fact it were not all right I wouldn't get more than a few yards. It was fairly bright in the parking area and when I walked across to the N.S.U. I would present a slowly moving target with good fore-lighting and a clear outline against the motel windows.

The more deserted a place appears the more it is peopled by the nerves and this could be discounted. Further, the headlights had been those of a car leaving, not arriving, and the two men had not gone out through the restaurant: the inference was that they had used a side-door, perhaps the one I had used. And finally: if they had wanted to deal with me they wouldn't both have gone up with Benedikt.

So I walked across to the N.S.U. and discounted another possibility as I went: there could be a third man waiting outside for me. That was just nerves again, stomach-think.

Brain-think: Benedikt had run it too close. They had come here to deal with him, not with me. He may have realized that when we had sat talking at the table. Being not only a potential defector but a double, he had broken down. In cases like his there is a defeat mechanism: the psychic system suddenly can't take any more because it's overloaded. Coming across to the other side presents a hazard comparable to jumping a chasm. It may be only a short jump but when you're in the middle of it you feel the onset of doubts, you distrust all the arguments that have driven you to the act. And you can't turn back.

This had been in Benedikt's face. The outward physical sign of psychic collapse.

The N.S.U. seemed all right. There would have been time for them to rig it, blow me up when I touched it. But that wasn't logical. Even so I held my overnight case in front of me when I opened the door, as a gesture of man's need to survive.

I hadn't checked out at the desk. They would find enough for the bill on the dressing table. (London is particular about things like that, and one fine day and with any luck the A-positive in Accounts would check with the Rhesus-negative in Mission Reports to confirm. They slang you harder for not paying bills than for trying to sting them for expenses.) It would make no difference to the motel manager, the fact of my not checking out conventionally. He would still have reported it as unusual if I had gone through the correct motions, because I'd given no prior indication of leaving tonight. Either way I would be suspect number one as soon as the police were told about Herr Benedikt. Apart from my sudden departure there were prints all over the room that tallied with those in my own. But the German police were thorough and would busy themselves also with suspects two and three. The one real problem was the N.S.U.: its Hanover matriculation was duly noted in the reception book.

But I couldn't telephone Ferris from the motel. The best idea was to use one of the emergency phones along the autobahn. Then I could peel off eastwards and head for Neueburg where Benedikt said there was the clockmaker.

Lights swung across from the road just as I started the engine and it was unsettling for an instant because it didn't have to be a rocking detonator: they could have connected it with the ignition. Any kind of disturbance – sudden moving light – can be unsettling when you're not certain it's just the ignition you're switching on, when you're ready to believe you can be switching on Kingdom Come.

But I didn't like it. You shouldn't have to justify being unsettled. If you think there's a bomb linked with the ignition key then don't touch the bloody thing.

Some people got out of the car that had swung off the road and I watched them cross to the motel. Then I moved off, heeling her over a bit on the springs to displace anything if it were there and have it done with. But everything was all right so I went on worrying because everything shouldn't be. When you get in their way they don't just leave you alone.

Between the motel and the filling station on the autobahn loop-road there was too much traffic to make observation worth while: the mirror was never clear of lights and I didn't do anything about it because it was only a two-lane strip and nobody would have wanted to overtake even if I'd invited them, with so much stuff coming the other way.

I wasn't sure how I was going to put it to Ferris, over a telephone. There was a lot I still didn't know about the Benedikt situation and all I could give him were the facts without throwing in any assumptions. Then he would have to tell London and they'd have an immediate baby. Ferris had said London wanted him badly: the contact, the man who'd told Lovett when the next Striker was going down. And now they couldn't have him. They would say I should have got him for them, kept him alive and sent him through, and they would be absolutely right. I might even have done that if the material had held up but the simple fact was that it hadn't. Benedikt had been dead before they took him upstairs and he would have been no use to the Bureau even if they hadn't put the cheese-wire on him.

It's happened before with people like Benedikt: they collapse internally and go on running like a headless chicken until someone switches them off or they do it for themselves as Lazlö did. Parkis wouldn't have got any sense out of Lazlö even if he hadn't swallowed the thing and hit the floor and Parkis had known it. That was why he was so annoyed.

It was an Esso station. There was enough on board for the run to Neueburg but I might have to go on from there and places in deeper country would be closed.

Anyway it was for Ferris to tell them. One of his functions was to keep London off my back.

'*Vierzig.*'

His hands were raw in the cold.

The stars were very clear and the moon was above the Harz Mountains, its outline sharp even on the eastern curve. The pump droned. A boy ran out from the building and sprayed the screen and began wiping it.

Did it go well, with the rotary engine? They both asked the same thing at the same time, and laughed. I said it went well. There weren't many RO-80s on the road yet and people were interested. The screen began shining.

Twenty litres had gone in by the time the Mercedes 300 pulled in behind. It could have come up on the other side of the pumps but apparently it didn't need petrol.

The boy went to see to him.

If it rained later tonight, the man said, the road would freeze. I said I didn't think it would rain, the moon was too clear.

The driver of the Mercedes had got out. I couldn't see his face because the overhead floods threw shadow from his hat-brim. He wanted his screen cleaned, he told the boy. Sound carried easily on the cold air. Was that all he wanted? That was all.

'Stop at twenty-five,' I said.

'Didn't you ask for forty litres?'

'Yes. But stop at twenty-five.'

We worked a lot of instinct. Sometimes it's all we have.

The pump stopped droning.

There was a second man in the Mercedes. He was just a vague shape behind the screen at the moment because the boy had sprayed it and hadn't wiped it yet. The engine was still running.

How about the oil?

I said he could check it. Instinct was wholly in charge now but confirmation was available. It would take longer for the man to check the oil than for the boy to finish the screen of the Mercedes and once it was finished they would tip him and drive away. But I didn't think they would do that.

The oil was all right, the man said.

I gave him a note and he went into the building for the change: they don't carry a cash-bag at night as they do in the daytime.

The boy was thanking the driver of the Mercedes and going towards the building. The Mercedes was black, an uncommon colour these days, rather old-fashioned, funereal. The man wore a black overcoat. He was getting into the car, not hurrying.

What I really wanted to do was to go a short distance along the autobahn and use an emergency phone to tell Ferris what had happened, so that he could pass it on to London. It was only reasonable: they'd knocked another hole in the fabric, first Lovett and now Benedikt, and London would expect a report on that, however brief. Then I wanted to peel off and take a minor road south-east and then make east for Neueburg.

Now things had changed and I could do a U-turn and go back the way I'd come, but they would certainly cling on and wait for an opportunity and then use it: the dark winding road would give them an advantage. In any case it wasn't what I really wanted to do.

They hadn't got on to me by luck. They must have driven out of the parking area (I had seen their lights) and waited by the side of the road in case I were going to scarper. If I'd stayed at the motel they would probably have arranged it that the end came for me peacefully in my sleep, though it seemed less likely. There were several pointers to a single supposition: their orders were to make it look like an accident. Otherwise they could have dropped me with one careful shot as I crossed from the motel to the car.

The man came out of the building.

'*Vierzig-fünfzig–sechzig.*'

I put the change away.

They'd gone in quickly for Lovett. It had been an emergency: a leak had been exposed. The best they could do was to fancy it up as a suicide. They'd worked as fast with Benedikt the moment they'd seen the light. He had been the leak itself. But with me they could take their time and make it look like an accident. Benedikt might have told me the lot or nothing: they weren't to know. But whatever I now possessed they were going to arrange that it would shortly amount to no more than a pattern of memory-traces fading on the surface of a dead cortex.

I looked once towards the Mercedes. Its shape was a black glitter under the glare of the floods and behind the screen their faces were white in contrast with their dark overcoats. The car was very clean and they were dressed with the correctness of pallbearers. They sat without moving, upright on the seats and with the patience of those who await a ritual.

I looked the other way along the perspective of the autobahn, a tapering ribbon of frost-grey under the moon.

They would have more speed than I and they were heavier but I got in and started up because this was the only road to where I had to go.

Chapter Nine

AUTOBAHN

'Ferris? I'm somewhere along the autobahn.'

He wouldn't say anything.

'I made contact. But it was no go.'

'Why not?'

'They broke the shepherdess. But I suppose London ought to know. Ought to be told.'

'Let me have the facts.'

'Well they went in quick for him and she's one thousand two hundred and ten kilos dry-weight, lighter than the 300, not critically but it's no use comforting yourself. They did it with some wire.'

'Where are they now?'

'I don't know. You can work the whole thing out to a formula and that's what I did. I don't mean when they went in for him. I mean when they came for me. And heavy. It was the heaviness that I didn't like.'

'Give me some more.'

'Are you listening, Ferris?'

I subscribe to Coué, Maltz and the Frenchman who said *si tu veux tu peux*. They all make the same point but Coué put it quite well: in any contest between the imagination and the will, the imagination always wins.

We've tested this out in training sessions using alcohol, electric shock techniques, artificially induced fatigue states and varying degrees of auto-hypnosis. An example would be: if the ship's been sunk under you and it's a ten-mile swim to the shore you'll stand more chance of getting there by using imagination instead of will-power. You can grit your teeth and will yourself to do it but the command is conscious and your *sub*conscious is on board for the trip and it can be a lead weight if it's left to its own little games: once it starts brooding about the black silent fifty-fathom void below your body the will-power is going to lose a lot of steam. But if you bring in the subconscious to work for you it means the imagination will be programmed in and in the place of a lead weight you've got yourself a propeller. Feed it the key-image 'shore' and you're there already, prone as a log and coughing up water but safe and alive.

Maltz confirms that the nervous system can't tell the difference between a real and an imagined experience. If this weren't true they could never produce a burn-mark on the back of the leg with an ice-cube by convincing the subject that it's a red-hot poker and they do it every day at St George's as a change from making tea.

The trick isn't fool-proof because so many other factors are in play: your personality patterns, state of mind, so forth. It only works with some people some of the time.

It didn't work with me when I took the N.S.U. away from the Esso station. My 'shore' was a telephone call to Ferris somewhere along the autobahn because if I ever made that call it would mean I'd ditched the bastards first. The one factor against my using the scheme was the situation itself: you've got time to spare in a steady crawl-stroke but with the RO-80 pitching it up through the gears and the arithmetic to work out it didn't give the imagination a one-track focus: imagination was needed to help size up the mechanics of the thing and that was why technical considerations kept merging in my mind with the telephone call to Ferris.

I let it go. The nervous system was going to have to do it the hard way instead of just homing in on a Ferris-sensitive target by preconditioned reflex. It was going to have to do what it was bloody well told to do.

I could feel – actually feel in my stomach and on my hands and the back of my neck – what the imagination was doing, or that part of it that I didn't need for mechanics. It was being frightened. And in an odd way.

I was less afraid of the chance of imminent death or hideous injury than of abstract things: blackness, heaviness – the surrealistic identities of the people behind me in the night. I was being hunted not by two men in a motor-car but by the dark-coming hounds of hell. Perhaps it was because they had looked so inhuman sitting there correctly on their seats, faceless in funeral clothes, nameless but for a number-plate. To put it more finely, this was not quite fear. It was dread.

They should have picked him up, sat him against the wall or something, not left him sprawled out staring at the bits of broken china. It had been indecent.

Their headlights came on suddenly in the mirror and I knew what was happening because I'd worked out the formula: the formula for survival. The basic data for the N.S.U. RO-80 included weight and speed figures: 1210 kilograms with a dry tank, 180 kilometres per hour. The gears were automatic and the front wheels did the driving. The time-lag was about the same with the automatic as with a manual shift and so it didn't make any difference. The superior traction of front-wheel drive wasn't likely to affect things even on the fast curves north of the mountains because there would have to be a curve that had to be *driven* round if the N.S.U.'s cornering advantages were to be brought into play.

The Mercedes 300 weighed 1560 kilos and the top speed was 190 k.p.h. Gear control was optional and I didn't know which this one had. The rear wheels did the driving.

First findings: all factors being equal the Mercedes could overhaul me by 10 k.p.h. and give me a 350-kilo nudge into the tree-trunks when it was ready.

Unknown data: the precise weight of the two men and the amount of fuel they had on board. There was nothing to be done about this. Give a man eighty kilos with shoes and overcoat: they had an extra 430. Assume their tank was close on full: it took them past 450. But it would need a slide-rule to decide the balance: how much their extra weight was going to cost them in acceleration and maximum speed, how much it was going to help them nudge me off the road.

I'd done what I could at the Esso station, telling the man to shut off at twenty-five litres. That amount would get me to Hanover if necessary and left the N.S.U. lighter.

Workable findings: assume the best figures – both men were heavy and their tank was full and it would cost them 10 k.p.h. in maximum speed. Add 1 k.p.h. In one hour there would be a kilometre's distance between us and with that kind of margin I could peel off at whatever loop-road I liked: Braunschweig Hildesheim, Hanover itself. And they wouldn't see me go. Assume, the worst figures – both men were average weight and they had a quarter tankful and they had the edge on me in terms of maximum speed. The extra weight of one man would bring down the speed fractionally but not the full 10 k.p.h.

Conclusion: the Mercedes had to be faster than the N.S.U. by 1 k.p.h. if they were going to stay with me and send me into the trees. I believed on the figures alone that it was 1 k.p.h. faster and that they could do that.

There was only the one area in which I could hope to work, hope to avoid a mathematical certainty. The N.S.U. had a rotary engine and was lighter by 350 kilos and that gave me the edge on them in acceleration. I was already establishing a lead: that was why they'd just put their headlights on. They were worried. Their idea would be to stay with me almost bumper-to-bumper with their lights out so that I couldn't see enough in the mirror to judge how close they were, couldn't see which side they were creeping up on to shape for the final nudge.

The N.S.U.'s superior acceleration and the Mercedes' higher top speed would vary the distance between us as we went north. It would be like a Chriscraft towing a water-skier on a long piece of elastic: the N.S.U. would draw ahead and then the tension would be taken up and the Mercedes would close the gap until it hit.

The only outside factor that could come into play was the presence of other cars making north. But we were both going to take it right up to the ceiling and there wasn't likely to be anyone driving in the 180–190 region at night.

The lights were good on the N.S.U. and the vision-field was flat, wide and clear of reflector-fault. The speed was moving through 135 when I took a look and the dipped lamps of the Mercedes were rising slowly to the top of the mirror as the gap widened. Then they switched to full beam and caught me across the eyes and I tilted the glass and drew into the middle area to wait for reaccommodation.

The autobahn ran dead straight in this section and the moon's glow defined it as far as the horizon. There was nothing to do yet except let the engine take her up to the maximum and hold her there. The one trick I could hope to pull off must be kept for emergencies and there weren't any emergencies for the moment. The first thing to do was test out the figures I'd been working on: if they were both heavy men and their tank was nearly full then I was going to consolidate the lead I already had on them and peel off as soon as I was out of sight. Then I would put a call through to Ferris while the engine cooled down.

Half a minute later the N.S.U. reached her maximum. The pointer just went up to the 180 k.p.h. mark and stayed there. With this engine there were no valves so there was no indication of bounce; it was purely a matter of starvation: the combustion-chambers were being swept at the speed above which the mixture didn't have time to go in.

The steering was still dead positive and when I moved the wheel a degree she came back correctly without any yawing. I couldn't test for brake-fade because I wanted to know if the 300 could close the gap. The cockpit was full of light but I couldn't tell if it were getting brighter: the reference was too vague.

The dread had passed. Perhaps it had been automatically set up by the organism in its own defence. The situation was dangerous and could be mortal but the necessity of working out the mechanics hadn't allowed the onset of normal fear: and a situation becomes more dangerous if there is no fear present to alert the nerves and prepare the body. Blood should be drawn to the internal organs, draining from the digestive and secretory glands and skin by contraction of the arterioles so that the heart, brain and muscles can be fed. Breathing should quicken so that the muscles can be given an oxygen reserve. The eyes should dilate, admitting more light.

The human body is no fool but these days it's a little old-fashioned: the defence mechanism set up to dodge the swing of a dinosaur's tail is less effective when life or death depends on the position of a needle on a speedometer. But I may well have been, by some small degree, better prepared for action now that the fit of dread was over. It had been the most the organism could do.

Within the next kilometre the first results came in: the light was stronger inside the cockpit and when I tilted the mirror the back-glare was painful. They were closing the gap.

It wasn't going to be so easy, ringing Ferris.

We passed a truck and I felt the slight air-buffeting as the slip-streams merged and just for an instant I took my foot off but it was already too late: I couldn't slow hard enough to take up a position in front of the truck and use it as a shield. The Mercedes would slot into the gap and the truck itself would become part of the pattern and I didn't want that because they wouldn't have any scruples. Even a twenty-ton twelve-wheeler could be sent off the road if the driver was baulked and I didn't know how hard the Mercedes was going to try when it came to the in-fighting. They had to make it look like an accident and an overturned truck wouldn't detract from appearances.

The inside of the N.S.U. went dark. They'd been overhauling me progressively at 5 or 6 k.p.h. and when I'd taken my foot off for an instant it had closed the gap and brought them right up and they'd cut their lights. The mirror showed a vague dark shape with the glint of chrome in the moonlight. Above the wind-rush I could hear their engine. The needle was steady on 180 and I drew to the crown so that I would have room to manoeuvre when they started.

There was the temptation to hit the brakes and make contact just to surprise them but at this speed it could be immediately lethal. We were covering a hundred yards in two seconds and if the huge weight of the Mercedes didn't make a direct strike on the fore-aft axis of the N.S.U. it would send it off-centre and no amount of steering would bring it back.

Perhaps they were expecting me to do something like that. They didn't mind how it happened, whether it was the result of action on their part or retaliation on mine: providing I jumped the crash-barrier in a series of barrel-rolls and finished up ablaze in the trees down there it wouldn't matter to them how it was done.

It looked very wide in the mirror, very black, a dark wave surging behind me. I was waiting for the nudge and I had to guess which side they'd go for. So long as it wasn't dead central it would work well enough: the smallest impact to one side would send me out of control.

Sweat began again but this was normal: I was in a trap and couldn't get out, couldn't go faster or slower or steer my way clear. A curve came and the crash-barrier uprights sent a flickering echo against the windows and then they made their first strike and the shock went through the body-shell into my seat and as soon as the line was corrected I felt for the safety-belt and clipped it home and set the driving-door to locked.

Far ahead in the moonlight a blob showed on the ash-white strip of the road and I hit the horns and kept them blaring because he was too near the crown and I couldn't slow: the next strike or the one after that would throw the whole thing wild and I didn't want to take anyone with me.

It was an Opel Rekord and he pulled over to let me through and then flicked his lights in protest. They made a feeble semaphore in the mirror with the reflection glancing off the mass of black cellulose behind me. Then they tried again and the sweat broke out because the N.S.U. was into a series of oblique lunges before I could correct. The headlamp beams swept the road with the slow regularity of windscreen-wipers and a shrill came from the tyres as traction tried to damp out centrifugal force. Something pattered on the body and hit the left side of the screen with the sound of sudden hail: the nearside front wheel was running off the edge of the concrete and fragments of gravel were shooting up clear of the wing, curving and falling into the slipstream.

Most of the control was re-established but I still needed the whole width of the road before I could get the steering back to straight-path conditions and even when I'd managed it there'd be no useful future because they'd only line up another strike as soon as I was steady so I pulled the only trick in the bag, the one I'd saved for emergencies.

The odds were one in three.

Along this stretch the road was three cars wide. The strip in the middle of the two lanes was rough grass with flood-water gullies each side. At the moment I was doing the expected: trying to kill out the oblique lunges and bring her straight again. The dark shape was still in the mirror but less distinct: possibly they were holding back in case one of my tyres burst under the strain of the yawing action. They wanted me off the road: they didn't want me to start breaking up in front of them. Their great weight, moving at great speed, could ram an obstacle effectively but if the N.S.U. were wheels-up or sliding on its side the deceleration-figures could force them against the screen.

If I had been running straight I could have deliberately set up this swinging action but that would be unexpected and they would have been warned. There wouldn't be another chance like this – with the N.S.U. swinging *expectedly* from one side to the other – unless they made a new strike and again failed with it. I didn't want to rely on that because they were getting their hand in now and the *coup de grâce* wouldn't be long in coming.

The whole operation depended on the mirror and on timing.

It was more difficult to do than I had thought. The little animal brain inside the back of my skull was snivelling about the risk. It would have liked the odds to be better than one in three.

Through the rhythmic series of swings the mirror went dark, light, dark, light as the N.S.U. crossed and recrossed the bows of the Mercedes and during the third or fourth light period I hit the brakes and felt the pull on the safety-harness as the speed came down and the tyres set up a long howling and I watched the mirror although there was no point in watching it because if it ever went dark again there'd be nothing else to do.

But it was all right. The 300 had been so close that it ripped metal off the side of the N.S.U. as its black shape came sliding past but the swing was already under control when the brakes had begun dragging and there was no more than a slight rolling on the springs. There was also one guaranteed factor in play: despite larger discs and tyres the Mercedes didn't have the stopping-power of the N.S.U. because of the difference in mass and this was so cheerful to think about that I threw in an added risk and cut the lights and hoped that the near-blackout would worry them more than it worried me: the balance of life or death could depend in the final analysis on liver and carrots.

The howling noise went on and I freed the discs a couple of times to break down the friction as the needle swung through the nineties and below. Their lights came on and I saw the big sil-houette still drawing away although it was under the brakes by now and slowing. Rubber-smoke began curling past my wind-screen in little clouds and then I stopped thinking about the 300 and concentrated on what had to be done next. The side-lamps had been left burning so that the facia was lit and I could read the speed because after five kilometres at 180 k.p.h. my normal visual judgement would be affected and true speed through the lower register would seem slower than it was and I didn't want to roll her when I turned.

There was a strong smell of rubber and asbestos by now but the braking effect had damped out the last of the swings and we were on a perfectly straight course a metre from the grass centre strip and when the needle dipped below 30 k.p.h. I released the brakes and made a three-quarter-lock turn across the soft ground and into the faint light flooding from a car that was coming south on this track. I was already accelerating through the sixties and tucked well in but the driver had been worried to see me broadside on across the road even in the distance and he went by fast with a lot of noise from the horn because in any case it was strictly *verboten* to drive across the centre strip like that.

By the time the N.S.U. was over the ton and still climbing I began trying to assess the chances but the basic data was so vague that I gave it up. It would mean having to work out how long it would take the Mercedes to slow up and how long it would take it to make the turn and close the gap again behind me on the north-south track. There had never been any question of foxing them: they would have got the rough idea the moment I braked, and the man who wasn't driving would have hung himself over the seat to see what I was doing. It was a question of using the only two advantages the N.S.U. had over the Mercedes on a straight run – acceleration and braking – and hoping to find some sort of peel-off point on this side before they closed up again.

I gave them something like three minutes.

There wasn't anywhere to turn off within that period and the obvious thing to go for was the loop-section where I'd taken on fuel. They would be big in the mirror before I could reach it but they might not succeed in knocking me off in time. The idea had only one advantage: there weren't any alternatives. The N.S.U. would be faster along winding roads but there would be other traffic and there was the risk of smashing up an innocent family because the big 300 was in business now and no one was safe. The only hope was to stay on the autobahn and use the elbow-room.

Light began filling the N.S.U.

They had been quick.

There wouldn't be another chance of pulling the same trick again if I let them come right up on me so if there were anything to do it had to be done now and I thought of something and did it and the tyres shrilled again as the brakes came on at full grip. I judged the gap to be still big enough to make the operation worth trying.

The speed was down to 30 k.p.h. when I turned on to the grass centre strip and felt the rear end break away and corrected it and brought her back in the opposite direction with my undipped heads catching the Mercedes full across the screen. I could see them clearly, their hands going up to shield their eyes, the big car veering a degree in the glare and the brakes hissing on. Then it came at me.

I was ready for it but the grass was soft and I was late getting away because of the wheelspin and the glancing blow slung the N.S.U. full circle and for a while I was just sitting there looking along the headlight beams watching them start an initial slide along the centre strip that carried them sideways for fifty metres with turf ploughing up in a wave over the roof before the momentum died and their wheels began spinning again for grip.

I was back on the concrete before they were but the gap was only medium and they were closing as hard as they could and I knew that somewhere inside the correct black overcoats and stiff white collars the semblance of an emotion had been provoked. Anger. From my limited information I assumed that their controllers had given orders that I should be killed and that my death should appear accidental, but they were finding it more difficult than it had seemed and now they were angry because their pride was hurt. They were no longer implementing an arrangement: they were conducting a duel.

They *wanted* to kill me now. It hadn't mattered to them before.

This could make a difference. Emotion at very high speed could lead to misjudgement. But it was my sole consolation. The light was already a glare inside the car before the last of the mud was centrifuged from the tyres and we settled down on the top-limit mark with the windrush blotting out most of the engine sound.

Then they cut their lamps so that I couldn't see which side they were going for. The mirror was only a frame for vague movement now, dark and shifting and inconsistent.

A bump came and I corrected the line but it wasn't too bad because they'd hit too close to the centre. Then they had another go and the impact was well to one side and very heavy and I did what I could but this time the strain dragged a tyre off and I watched the headlamp beam go spilling across the edge of the road and flooding down into woodland. The N.S.U. was airborne for a few seconds, floating strangely among light and shadows, then it struck rubble and began pitching and I saw the trees coming and turned the engine off before the night went wild.

Chapter Ten

FUGUE

The moon gleamed, set in shadows.

Shapes, but not of trees or smashed metal: I expected shapes of trees. The moon was glass-bright, translucent, shimmering, sometimes going dark and emerging again among the shadows.

'Wait a minute.'

The whole of the organism was prepared to arrange its survival if it could: run, fight, beat out flames, bind blood in with a tourniquet, free itself from wreckage. The components were immediately available: nerve, sinew, gas-interchange process, adrenalin supply. Intelligence alone was absent. The organism had to be told what to do, and nothing knew.

The moon, alive with light, held a globe of colour in its centre: blue. And in the centre of blue was another globe, totally black.

The shapes were fainter, touches of light on cloud, the cloud silver, curling, hanging near the moon, a line dividing its softness. A feather lying curved above the moon.

'Who are you?'

The moon darkened again and shone again and watched me. It was an eye watching me.

'*Bitte*?'

There was pain in the organism but not enough to limit movement. I was on one elbow looking across at her face, recognizing it but not recalling it, knowing I had seen it before but not knowing where or when.

Information came flooding in so fast that the receptor areas couldn't cope with it but I saw now that there was light coming from behind her, from the street, and that something reflected it so that her eye shone. Then there was an implosion of random images and within a millisecond the whole scene was formed and took on significance: she was sitting hunched in a chair near the bed where I lay and tears had dried on her face.

'Who are you?' I said it in German this time.

She told me her name but paramnesia is odd: recognition is present but recall can't just be switched on like that. The name meant nothing when she said it.

A young face with amethyst eyes swollen from crying, a bewildered mouth. All her attention was on me. There were no trees or shattered glass, no flames to beat out. Sweat began trickling from my temples and I stopped making an effort, suddenly aware that the effort I had been making was enormous and very desperate because I was scared sick of seeing the lot go, the whole lot.

The only hope was in taking the pressure off, letting the neural traces show up under the hypo in their own good time. I didn't use English any more: the one word she had spoken had been in German.

'Is there any kind of head injury?'

My hands were moving about, the fingers hunting for blood. Quite a lot of the organism was coping well enough, doing its best to look after itself.

She said something but I wasn't interested: there was so much data coming in that I wanted to sort it out before anything new was presented. A window and the unlit lamp and of course her face and various colours and the tear stains.

'Oh yes,' I said and sat still for a bit. Traces were showing up: I had seen tears on her face before when she'd said she hated me and that I was impotent. 'So that's who you are.'

Memory, returning, can't present every detail because there are too many. Putting your clothes on you don't observe the pattern of the tweed or the style of the shoes: you simply know that these are *your* clothes. It's not a matter of Striker, shepherdess, Wagner, cheese-wire, Benedikt, ignition switch plus several million other images and their significance. It's a matter of finding yourself back in a *place* composed of all the things you have ever known. Identity.

'Wait a minute.' I was sitting on the edge of her bed, head in my hands. It would need a minute to settle in. If you don't take it easy the whole thing can go blank again.

'Nitri,' she said again, frightened.

'Yes I know. Yes.'

Her scent. It had been inside the car. The N.S.U.

There was still an area of darkness and I was aware of it but it would have to be left alone. Some kind of inhibitory block, repression of unpleasant events.

'What time is it, Nitri?'

'Four.'

'Night?'

'Yes. But you – '

'When did I get here?'

'In the night.'

'Hours ago – *this* night? Come on – some hours ago?'

'You said you were coming.'

Blank. It didn't fit anywhere. She had sounded frightened. Perhaps I'd spoken too loudly. That was because I was frustrated: there might be a need for hurry and I couldn't.

'Don't worry,' I told her.

I sat blanking my mind for as long as a minute and it worked and I got a completely lucid sequence: the telephone cold in my hand, the sweep of light as a car went by, the smell of the exhaust-gas. *I'm coming to see you*. Pain across the shoulders and chest *What happened?* A loose feeling in one shoe. *I'll be there in an hour*. A car slowing or seemingly slowing so that I dropped back into the shelter of the woodland.

'I was phoning from the autobahn. I just wanted to know if you'd be alone.'

'I'm always alone.'

She meant always without Franz.

Her body was milky under the nightgown and the light from the street shadowed her eyes. She asked me why I had come.

I couldn't tell her. They might already have found him on the floor and the number of the N.S.U. was in the reception-book and there was an N.S.U. with that number lying smashed in the trees near the autobahn. So I couldn't have gone back to the motel or checked in at any hotel in Linsdorf or Hanover or anywhere at all, looking like this. There was no safe-house because I was

81

working with prescribed cover: Walter Martin attached to Accidents Investigation Branch temporary overseas location Weserbergland Federal Republic Germany. The A.I.B. was an official organization in the pursuit of lawful business in co-operation with a foreign government and if anything irregular happened to Walter Martin the A.I.B. must be protected from any consequences. The Bureau would want to take care of this situation before it could get out of hand so I had to tell Ferris as soon as I could. The trouble was that I'd blown my own cover and couldn't go near the Linsdorf base or the A.I.B. unit or Ferris himself. I'd had to find a bolt-hole and go to ground and this was the only place but I couldn't tell her that.

'I needed you,' I said.

'People don't need me.'

She meant Franz didn't.

'I had an accident.'

She let herself laugh suddenly. 'Did you?'

The Special Uses sheepskin coat was ripped and one shoe was loose, split right across. I didn't know what my face looked like but the wound in my hand had been opened up and they were both caked with earth.

Another clear sequence began and I sat with it as if I watched a film: the trees coming up in a wave at great speed as the car lurched into a slow roll, still airborne and then hit rubble and plunged with the headlights turning the scene into an abstract kaleidoscope pattern of black and white, the trees winter-bare and resembling a gigantic stack of driftwood bursting and hurled against the windscreen, the percussion of wood on metal and glass and the white hail as the screen went, the scene revolving slowly at first until it was upside down and then jerking as the saplings bent under the onslaught and sent the car sideways and straight and sideways again and pitching lower into the undergrowth while the momentum was broken against stripped white bark and I kept my knees jack-knifed and my feet on the crash-cushion, the reek of fuel from a torn pipe and sometimes the glow of the moon spinning through black branches and always the bite of the straps holding my body back while my head's own weight dragged at the neck and tried to break it. Everything suddenly still.

'Don't worry,' I said again.

'I was scared.'

'I know.'

'You didn't recognize me, I mean.'

'I do now.'

She slid off the chair and knelt in front of me and I made to touch her face to reassure her but my hand was scabbed with dried blood and she was clean and young and fragile in the aureole of the street's light and I took my hand away.

'Do you need a doctor?'

'No. Why were you crying?'

'I was thinking about Paul and I suppose I went to sleep. It was late when you phoned. Paul Dissen. You know it was his plane today? He — '

'Yes.'

'He got mixed up in my dream, half himself and half Franz, it was grotesque. Dead, of course,' She got up and looked helpless for a moment, floating in the light from the window, aimless. 'He's always dead when I dream about him. I'll fetch some water.'

I decided to recognize the fact that retrograde amnesia was blocking off part of the past. I didn't want to telephone Ferris until I could give him the whole thing. I remembered most of the post-crash sequence, leaving the N.S.U. and finding an emergency phone and later going down through the trees again and reaching the secondary road and stopping a truck, waving a handful of deutschmarks in the glare of his lights. But I didn't know why I had crashed the N.S.U. because the retrograde kick covers a period of anything up to fifteen minutes prior to concussion and the last thing I could remember was a man at an Esso station saying if it rained later tonight the roads would freeze. I said I didn't think it would rain because the moon was too clear.

It happens with a lot of people – drivers, airline pilots – and there's nothing they can do about it when there's an enquiry: they just 'don't remember what happened'. It is why Stirling Moss couldn't explain what made him crash. The memory traces need time to consolidate and store experience and if the head gets a blow it's like tapping a bowl of sand just after someone has drawn figures on it with a stick: it smooths over.

She was bathing my hands. I could have done it for myself in the bathroom but she'd got it all set up with towels on the carpet and hot water in the bowl and I didn't stop her because playing dolls would help her to deal with the fright and bewilderment: she'd been dreaming about Paul-Franz being dead and then I'd come through the doorway and fallen flat on my face with delayed shock and it must have been hard for her to take.

'I never see him in a plane or in a wreck or anything. You'd think I would.'

'Yes.'

She had a whole plastic bag of cotton wool and tore bits off it

83

the wrong way, tugging at it and not getting anywhere. 'I see the funeral, men in black with pale faces I can't recognize. It's always a civilian funeral, I suppose because that's the only kind I've ever seen, my mother's, with big black cars and flowers. And all the time I'm thinking about the plane – it's made another widow and this time it's me.'

There had been a boy washing the windscreen of the N.S.U. He'd asked about the engine, if it ran well. The edge of the blank area was somewhere there: at the Esso station.

'You'll mess yourself up, Nitri.'

The water was red-brown in the bowl. She nodded and went to change it. I got up and followed her because this needed an entire bathroom and anyway I wanted to see if anything had happened to my face. But there must have been some kind of memory trace in the subconscious: the moment the N.S.U. had come to rest with the front lodged at an angle between two trees I'd snatched at the buckle and thrown the straps clear, kicking at the driver's door and finding it was jammed solid, dragging myself through the white fragmented windscreen and slitting a shoe on the frame. There was a branch in the way and my coat was catching but I forced myself through the gap with my scalp shrinking and goose-flesh everywhere: there was some kind of fear driving me on, pushing me through a gap that would have been impossibly small if the fear hadn't given me the strength. Not quite fear: a kind of dread.

'I'll make you a tourniquet from something.'

The water span red in the basin.

Full consciousness hadn't come back until I'd felt the telephone cold in my hand. The concussion would have left me trapped inside the wreck: i t was the dread that had taken over. I had known that unless I could get away from the wreck, something would come for me there. Even when I'd finished talking to her on the emergency phone there was no let-up: a car was slowing along the autobahn and I dropped down the earth bank and clawed my way through bramble and gone on across a knoll of trees. At one time headlights had swung through the higher branches as if a car were being turned, and the frost glittered on the dead leaves underfoot. Then there was the truck, much later, on the minor road, and my hand full of deutschmarks, waving.

The data was limited enough but it would have to do.

She was watching me in the mirror. My face wasn't too bad now that I'd rinsed off the earth. I'd obviously fallen somewhere or gone down the bank from the autobahn face first.

'There's a doctor in this block.' She was impatient, annoyed at her own sense of helplessness. 'There's nothing I can do for you.'

I said: 'I need a phone.'

Code-intro for the mission was sapphire needle and we cleared on it and didn't bother with anything else because it was fool-proof: if one of us were under duress we'd slip in the alarm-phrase and take it from there. The only danger was from bugging but he was very good on security and no one could have known I'd show up here.

'I've blown my cover.'

'All right.' There was sleep still in his voice but he'd said it straight away and I knew there'd been no need for any kind of code-intro because only Ferris would say 'all right' without hesitation when you phoned him three hours before dawn to tell him a thing like that. It wasn't the work involved that would upset him – all I wanted were some new papers and something to drive in – but the background inference: you don't blow your own cover unless you've got into a very dodgy position.

'How soon can you fix me up?'

'It depends where you're going.'

'Nowhere special.'

She had gone into the bedroom and shut the door but she could listen through it if she wanted to and I thought she probably would because the normal thing to do when you've had an accident is to call round at the nearest hospital for bandages and I'd shown up here and fallen all over the floor.

'What happened,' he asked. The sleep had gone from his voice. I didn't answer right away and he said: 'We're all clear.'

The throbbing across the shoulders and chest had set in again because I was standing up. The international-standard belt is designed to take 30 g's and the one in the N.S.U. must have absorbed nearly that amount of load and it was a wonder the slack hadn't whiplashed the buckle free. The only thing it hadn't done was to keep my head off the body-shell above the windscreen and the only reason there wasn't any blood was because the visor was padded.

'They got at the contact.'

'I see.'

I felt vaguely sorry for him. He'd told me that London wanted to know fully urgent who made contact with Lovett. For a moment I expected him to order a rendezvous. He'd have to do an awful lot of chasing about in the next few hours trying to help London deal with the blown cover thing and he'd probably go down to Linsdorf himself to stop any flap inside the A.I.B., but when half a mission hangs on a stable cover and the other half on getting a contact across and the cover's blown and the contact's dead it's reasonable for the director to ask for a meeting person-to-person if only so that he can tread on his agent's face.

I waited till he said something else. Five minutes ago he'd been asleep and now he was having to do a lot of thinking. And there was the third thing I had to tell him and I didn't want to do it until he'd had a chance to stop reeling.

'Where are you?'

'Where I was last night.'

On the other hand there is always a risk in meetings. The agent is usually infectious: there are tags at his back or trying to trace him or set up a trap and if he's seen making a contact it exposes the director. They are not two members of a team: they are strictly departmentalized. The agent is a bit of clockwork on the floor and when it hits something or turns over the director's hand comes down and sets it going again on a straight course unless it's broken in which case he throws it away and sends for another one. An agent can go through a mission and be set running again through another one and if he's lucky they can use him half a dozen times before they have to plug him with platinum tubing and bone-rivets or reach for the next-of-kin form. But the director is a career man, a white-collar manipulator who keeps his nails clean, stacking up mission after mission till they pension him off to prune roses.

'How much can you say?'

The door was shut and her English was school-level and we had our own terms for things and if I spoke fast there wouldn't be any risk. I knew two things about Nitri: she was at this moment completely safe and if anyone ever told her that she could possess Franz exclusively by selling her soul to the devil she would become totally dangerous.

'It's all right this end. It's just a question of bugs.'

He was silent for a bit and I knew he was considering a rendez-vous and the trouble was that we didn't have a safe-house in Hanover: there was no need for one because I was still too mobile and the mission had been running for only three days and every time we picked up some kind of direction the bastards blocked it. Lovett. Benedikt.

He said at last: 'What happened?'

'His code-name was Benedikt. He'd started doubling so as to get across and he didn't have the stamina. You know how it goes. There's the odd patch of info missing but I can guarantee that a few hours before he found out who I was he had to save himself.

He must have shown his hand and they didn't like him tagging me down to Linsdorf so he told them to come and get me. Then he broke up and went religious and tried to save me instead. Maybe he just confessed: it looked like that. They wiped him out. He knew they would.'

'Was it effective or did you have to break your way out?'

'It could have been effective. He drew them off me. But I was too interested. They did it in his room at the motel.'

He didn't say anything for a minute because he was partly thinking and partly listening for bugs. I supposed he would have been hysterical if he'd known the girl was so close because he was a fanatic about security. There's a story at the Bureau, very shop-worn by now: 'I saw old Ferris having a cup of tea with his mother in Lyons today. He had her screened first, of course.'

'And?'

'They had a go at me afterwards.' He had enough on his plate already without my telling him I'd lost my memory and anyway it must have happened: I don't just drive clean off the bloody road, I've passed my test and everything. There was probably some 9-mm material stuck in the tyres if anyone wanted to look for it.

'What happened to the cover?'

'I had to make a search in his room to see if they'd missed anything. There'll be prints. Then I had to get out. As soon as they find him I'll be first suspect.'

'Oh, shit.'

Because that had been the third thing I'd had to tell him. To-morrow there'd be a full-scale manhunt for Walter Martin throughout West Germany and although there was nothing to connect him with a non-existent government department in the U.K. it wasn't going to be easy for Ferris to fix me up with a new cover when the Identikit version of my face was plastered all over the papers.

But it wasn't my fault. Even if there's been time to do the search according to the book I couldn't have gone into my own room to fetch gloves because I'd been pretty sure they were waiting for me there. And I couldn't have stayed in the motel because everyone's got a right to go on living.

'Look,' I said, 'forget the cover.'

Rather stiffly he said: 'If you want one you can have one.' He really was very upset.

'Just get me some papers and if I'm stopped I'll play it by ear. Some papers and transport.'

'Where do I pick up the old one?'

'You don't have to. I wrote it off along the autobahn.'

'Hurt yourself?'

'There's a bit of a twinge in one tooth.'

'Don't mess me about – what sort of condition are you in?'

'Look, if I weren't capable of looking after myself I'd bloody well say so and if you get London to send in a shield I'll pull his balls off.' But I wasn't pleased about it and he knew that. I was protesting too much. It was a simple fact that if anyone broke in here at this moment my chances would be some degrees worse than fully normal because the right upper forearm was still in the healing stage and the left hand wanted stitches and the rib-cage and shoulders were bruised. But I had to be practical: if I had to start relying on a shield I'd take less care and that would be dangerous because even if they sent the best man in the Bureau he wouldn't be a hundred per cent reliable. No one is. It was no go.

'When do you want it by?'

He meant the papers and transport and I relaxed again. He wasn't going to press the shield thing. I said:

'Soon.'

After a bit he said: 'I'll put the keys in the mail-box and the papers will be in the car.'

'Don't do that. Leave it halfway along the Marienwerderstrasse.'

My left arm was aching because I was having to keep it raised. I thought of asking him to do something about shoes but it might hold things up and I was working on the premise that the Kriminalpolizei would be putting out a general alert from first light onwards. I watched the keyhole of the bedroom door all the time but there was never movement against it.

'All right,' Ferris said. 'It's a dark-blue Ford 17M, Hanover-registered. You'll find everything inside but don't forget if you're stopped: you've borrowed it.'

'As long as it's left-hand drive.'

'What've you broken?'

'I just like that kind. They don't attract attention.'

There might have been an edge of annoyance in his voice but I couldn't be sure. The right ear is unused to telephones. 'Can you give me any kind of location?'

They hate not knowing where you are and it's understandable because if you stop reporting they start getting the wind up and there's nothing they can do: you could be making progress somewhere inside an adverse area with no available communications or you could be at the bottom of the Mittellandkanal wrapped in a chain and London is pettish about sending a replacement unless the director in the field can practically produce a certificate, and this is reasonable too because a mission can get very sensitive in the final stages and there's a risk of rocking the boat. They'd thought Houseman was inside a burnt-out helicopter on Mont Blanc when the Lausanne thing was running and when they sent in a replacement the vibration was felt as far away as London and it nearly brought the Lowry off the wall.

'I'm going to have a try at reaching X.'

'All right,' he said.

'2-11-14-11-9-14-4-7.' He didn't ask for a repeat and he didn't question the need for speech-code because there can always be bugs. The second thing I knew about Nitri made it advisable and in any case the idea of putting your next location into so many words on a telephone brings out a rash.

The last thing he said was: 'Did you leave anything in the wreck?'

'The odd bit of skin. What the hell do you think I am?'

We were both a bit touchy: he'd got a week's work to do in half a day and I had to drive a hundred and fifty kilometres through a manhunt in daylight. I dropped the receiver with a bit of noise but the keyhole didn't change and there was no sound from the extension unit in the bedroom. This was no more than routine, like an actor checking his flies in the wings.

When I went in she was wrapped in the sheepskin coat and gazing into the glass. The room smelt of pear-drops.

'I've done some invisible mending.'

It was a perfect fit. The milky glow of her body was hidden by the scarecrow folds and she was shapeless: but the metamorphosis had meaning. It was the gesture that fitted so precisely. She had wrapped the coat around herself without thinking: not for comfort or warmth but to invest herself with the magic powers of its owner, just as the fledgling warrior girds himself in the lion-skin of a warlord in the ritual of his initiation, drawing into his sinews the strength of the mighty. Nitri, half-disguised, had become Nitri naked: lost, afraid, vulnerable to the threat of a bell's ringing and to the far explosion she would hear a hundred times before she heard it once.

'It looks new again,' I said.

'Did you talk to Paul Dissen yesterday?'

'Yes.'

It was a peach-tinted glass and her amethyst eyes were darker, indigo.

'Did you find out anything?'

'Quite a lot.'

'*He'll* never do that.' She meant Franz would never bale out.

_ 'He'll never have to.'

She let the coat fall away. 'You're finding things out all the time.'

'We all are.' The crash-analysis engineers, the aviation psychologists, the people with the magic power to stop Franz getting killed.

I didn't think much of my chances. The mission had only been running three days and we'd been blocked twice and all I'd managed to snatch out of the limbo was a name on a map. Neueburg.

She helped get my left hand through the sleeve and made me a tourniquet out of a scarf. The top of the nail-varnish bottle had fallen and I picked it up and she stuck it back although the bottle was empty: there'd been five or six gashes in the sheepskin.

'I want to see you again,' she said.

'You'll see me again.'

Chapter Eleven

THE HARE

It was one of those buildings without a soul, a sorting-house for displaced persons, its design so modern that it set a trend that would never be followed: there is something already old-fashioned about black-and-teak matt mouldings and mushroom chairs. Glass is a precious material that can make a palace of a cave, playing with light and casting it into shadowed places, but there is no real point in constructing an entire building of it to prove that here we have open minds and hold no secrets: the purpose is defeated by over-exposure and the result is that here we must shut our faces since we cannot shut our doors.

People moved through the place as if through the cross-section of a termitarium under glass. But they were very efficient.

The *Frau Doktor* i/c night-hours casualties was a big-boned lesbian with flat expressionless eyes and hands like a mechanical grab. She put in seven sutures and ordered anti-tetanus but that was as far as I would go with her: the capsules were livid-hued and presumably anti-bacterial and coagulation agents and I slipped them into my pocket when her head was turned and just drank the water which was refreshing. She obviously hadn't heard about indiscriminate sensitization and I didn't bother to tell her that I could produce enough antibodies to stop a mad horse given a fair chance.

They wanted me to fill in forms before discharging me because I still looked like an accident case and the Polizeidirektion would expect details so I asked if I could sit down while I filled them in and then edged out to the street when they were busy rubbing antennae with some remote inmate via the automatic switchboard.

It had cost me forty-five minutes but my hand would have been useless with the wound still open and the delay had to be written off as an investment. First light was an hour and a half away and even if they'd found Benedikt by now they probably wouldn't notice the remains of the N.S.U. until morning.

I had told Ferris to leave his 17M in the Marienwerdestrasse because it was just round the block from the hospital and it saved me having to walk back to the Lister-Platz. I slipped the match from under the wiper and got in. The keys were in the ignition and the tank was full and it only took half a minute to find the envelope under the back carpet. It was a big one, quarto.

Karl Ernst Rödl, Hamburg, Herrenhäuserstrasse 15 *geboren Hamburg* 1924, *Automechaniker.*

I hadn't had to tell Ferris I needed German-national papers: he knew they'd be looking for an Englishman. The rubber stamping bore faint segments and the photograph was sufficiently unlike my face to be natural but the *Automechaniker* bit was off key because my nails weren't normally split or ingrained. They slipped up sometimes in Credentials and Ferris would be on to that: a blast would already be working its way through his particular pipeline.

There was also a folder inside the envelope. *Chronological and Geographical Statistics Breakdown on Pattern-Crashes and Background Information on Dead Pilots.* All neatly typed and typical Ferris: he'd never use 'Stats' or 'Info'. It was what I'd asked him for last night and I put it straight into a pocket because if I ever had to leave the 17M as fast as I'd left the N.S.U. there wouldn't be time to clean up inside for inspection and the Kriminalpolizei wouldn't expect Karl Ernst Rödl to interest himself in Striker-crash statistics in English.

A pencilled note was at the foot of the folder. *Did you see what happened to Field Marshal Stöckener and Minister of Interior von Eckern? Watch this space!*

I got out and reached under the back of the car and scraped the nails of my right hand over the final-drive casing and got back in and wiped the worst off the finger-tips on the underside of the carpet. Then I started the engine.

So the *Feldmarschall* hadn't just skidded and the *Bundesminister* hadn't just taken a boy into the cloakroom. Benedikt had known: 'They are toppling in high places.' And Ferris had known: 'This time it's a rather big show.' And of course Parkis had known. The only one who hadn't known was the ferret down the hole and now he was being told.

I wondered why. It wasn't just a giggle behind the hand: Ferris would only tell you what he thought you needed to know. But he was running true to form and giving it to me in homeopathic doses and I wasn't going to think about it now: there were more pressing considerations and while the engine was warming I looked them over.

Findings: (1) It must have been the two men at the motel, the hot operatives who had gone into neutralize Benedikt. They must have tagged me from there as far as the autobahn and then had a go on the long dark sectors where no one would hear any shots. They would certainly have stopped when they saw the N.S.U. smashing up and they would have tried to go down among the trees to finish me off if I were still breathing but I'd got away from the wreck so fast that they couldn't find me: it may well have been a matter of seconds. (There had been headlights across the higher branches so they had probably been going so fast that they'd had to turn back.)

(2) A passing motorist might have seen me crash and stopped to see if he could help in which case he would have kept the adverse party away. If they hadn't been able to look inside the wreck they would now believe I was dead or so badly creased that I was out of the running. But this assumption had so little value as to be dangerous: a passing motorist would have telephoned the autobahn police patrols and they'd be called in anyway as soon as it was light enough for someone to notice the mess in the trees. The Bonn Telex would be putting out Mystery-Driver-Vanishes-from-Crashed-Car signals before noon today, nationwide. It was safer to assume the adverse party believed I was alive or would be informed at any time. They would continue to look for me and the police hunt would be thrown in as extra.

(3) The ferret was still in fair shape but the hole was now virtually a *cul-de-sac*. I was blocked off from Hanover, Linsdorf and all communications with people who had accepted me up to now as, *persona grata*: Philpott of A.I.B., Dr Wagner, Röhmhild, Boldt, Dissen and the rest of the Striker pilots. (Add Nitri from the time she saw the noon editions. I didn't know if she would go to the police when she heard they wanted me but I didn't think so: she had a curious interest in me either because I was probably

the only man ever to have turned down the chance of a novel experience or because she believed I could find the answer to the Striker problem before it killed Franz.)

The engine was warm and I checked my few belongings. At the hospital they'd given me back the silk scarf that had been round my arm as a tourniquet: it was a vaguely Freudian design and very Nitri. It was already in my pocket and it could stay there because I didn't want the police to find anything that could lead them to her if I had to abandon the car. The good *Frau Doktor* had fixed my arm in a sling so that my stitched hand couldn't fidget about and I took the thing off and stowed it in the sheepskin coat because during an interrogation you can conceivably keep a bandaged hand out of sight and when they'd tallied the number of the N.S.U. with the number in the motel register they'd be looking for someone in poor condition and a sling would be a positive advertisement.

At eighty-odd minutes before dawn in a wintry street I should have been prey to depression: mentally I was sound except for a patch of retrograde amnesia that couldn't be critical to the mission but physically I would have less chance than normal if anyone came for me close in and I didn't like that. Ferris had set me running and after three days I'd had to report that I'd blown my cover and lost the contact and become first suspect in a murder hunt and I didn't like that either. The opposition had twice tried to smear me out and Parkis was so scared at the size of this show that he wanted to stick a shield on to me so if they tried a third time one of two things would happen: either it would be successful and too late for a shield or Parkis would panic and insist on my having one in which case I'd tell Ferris that if I couldn't work alone he could signal London for a replacement and pull me out. Then some snivelling bitch at the Bureau would slide her scummy teacup off the Progress Report and scrawl *Mission Unconcluded* against my name and I liked that least of all.

But as I closed the driving window and shut myself in with the smell of ether and nail varnish and turned the car to face southwards I was elated instead of depressed. I had changed my cover and my nationality and I was on my own now with every man's hand against me throughout the whole country. From this time on I would follow the ways unknown to other men, digging my own dark tunnels as I went.

There was more stuff along the autobahn, mostly trucks, but I was south of Göttingen before dawn. I went fast and the mirror was clear for a hundred kilometres except once when I thought there was a dark shape drifting in it but it must have been a trick of the light and I never saw it again. Some rain had fallen this side of the mountains and the trees stood wet with it, their branches interlaced with silver in the headlights. Once a hare ran obliquely across my path, its coat already winter-white and its shadow bounding ahead until it found a gap and leapt beautifully, ears flat and feet together, vanishing. It was the only time I slowed, except when a rash of rearlights spread through the dark towards the Münden loop-road and I saw the police lamp swinging.

It was well organized: they expected fast motoring along this stretch and though the 17M was piling on through the 130s I didn't fetch any squeal from the treads pulling up. There were two long-haulers and a private V.W. standing in a queue, with some police cars drawn in on the margin. Of course there had always been this consideration: the choice when I'd left Hanover had been to make a really fast run and reach Neueburg with as little daylight driving as possible or take it slowly and allow a chance of dodging a police block by trying to see them before they saw me. It would have been practicable at a slower speed to pull up quietly with the lights doused and do a soft-shoe turn and get the hell out, give or take a few degrees of luck.

I had opted for the fast run on the assumption that nobody would find Benedikt before daylight at the earliest and that when they did find him there'd be a decent time-lag before the Kriminal-polizei were notified and the motel manager gave them the name and description of the *Engländer* who had joined the deceased for his last meal and had since left without checking out at the desk. I'd made the wrong decision, even in that moment of elation when my faith in myself had burned brightly in the surrounding gloom.

The one on signalling duty just pointed a gloved hand at the queue and I closed up on the rearmost truck, leaving the engine running. If he told me to switch it off I would switch it off but on principle I left it the way it was because if there's a chance in a thousand you might as well be ready to take it.

Probability: the manager had gone up to see if he could do anything for Benedikt soon after I'd left. He'd been worried about him during dinner: '*He looked ill. Is he all right?*' That would have brought the K.P. into the picture long before I'd reached Nitri's apartment but they wouldn't have decided on road-blocks until a bit later. Coming south from Hanover I had passed Linsdorf five kilometres to the west and was now heading away from it. That was why there hadn't been a police trap until now: they expected Martin to be moving *away* from the scene of the killing. There was probably another trap north of the Linsdorf loop-road along that side of the autobahn and I had passed it but not seen it because of the anti-dazzle screens along some sections of the centre strip.

It was a cold-storage truck standing in front of me, Frankfurt-registered: *Vollmond Gesellschaft*. Twelve delineation lights and the company's trade-mark: a full moon framing a laughing pig, so happy to be knifed in the *abattoir* and minced into sausages for the friendly bipeds to eat.

'Your papers, please.' Local, by his accent.

A cloud of diesel gas spread out from the long-hauler at the head of the line as it lumbered away. The uniformed figures stood half-obliterated.

I gave him my papers.

If the probability were correct and the manager had in fact gone up to see if he could do anything for Benedikt he might have decided to knock on my door – it was only the third along – for the sake of immediate human company because he would have been white and shaking by that time, or he'd thought I might have some sort of clue about what had happened since I'd been dining with Benedikt only half an hour ago. It could have started from there: Herr Benedikt dead and Herr Martin missing. *Polizei!*

'When were you born?'

'17 February, 1924.'

He was young and very military, keeping his head up and holding my identity card straight in front of him, only his eyes going down to read it.

'Where?'

'Hamburg.'

Glare began bouncing off the back of the truck and the laughing pig was slowly lost in it. The shadow of the patrolman appeared there like a gaunt secretary-bird, black and beakless. His colleague with the lamp hurried past and the sound of nearing thunder came from behind me and the light grew strong in the mirror.

'Switch off your engine please.'

I switched off my engine.

His torch clicked on and the beam caught me full in the face. What with that and the glare off the truck and the mirror I felt we were about ready for camera.

The thunder rolled loudly and there was a crash of gears. It sounded like a fifteen-tonner with trailer to match and I began wondering if he'd manage to pull up in time because if he chose this moment to leak some hydraulics I'd be no better off than the laughing pig, crushed, minced and canned in one labour-saving operation.

The torch-beam flickered back to my papers and then on to my face again and I grasped at a small hope: he was less efficient than he looked because if you shine a torch full into someone's face his eyes are going to screw up and they won't be screwed up in the photograph. He might make other mistakes.

A monstrous hiss came from the long-hauler and then the brakes dragged again and there was the shunt of heavy couplings. He'd dipped now and I could see better. What I could see most was the shine on the patrolman's holster just about eye-level from where I sat. He turned as another one walked up, an older man in *Hauptmann's* uniform, very smart-looking and big in the body, his head like a sculpted rock. They stood looking at my papers and suddenly I was unnerved and it had nothing to do with them.

I had missed a trick and that wouldn't do, it wouldn't do at all. The subconscious had been working busily during the crisis and now it presented its findings. Cancel all probabilities: it *hadn't* been the motel manager or anything to do with him. It had been the adverse party and this was their third try: they'd stopped my run at this section of the autobahn as surely as if they'd set up an ambush.

The front of the long-hauler filled the mirror and the lights went out. Voices. The diesel clattered to silence. Ahead of me the group of police stood back and the Volkswagen pulled away.

They *had* managed to go down into the trees and look inside the wreck of the N.S.U. and when they saw it was empty they'd beaten around a bit and then gone up and used the nearest emergency phone and told the Kriminalpolizei to check on an *Engländer* named Martin who had been staying at the motel in Linsdorf where a man named Benedikt was now lying dead in his room. They should also check up on his car which they would find alongside the autobahn. The informant's name was Schmidt and he was telephoning in the interests of justice. It had begun *then*.

I didn't know how much sleep I'd had in Nitri's apartment after I'd passed out: it wouldn't have been more than four or five hours and it had been recuperative and not restorative but that was no excuse for missing a trick on this scale. Instead of being so perversely content that every man's hand would soon be against me I should have assumed it was against me *already*: should have assumed the people who had finished Benedikt would automatically try to pull off a double by sounding the alarm before I got too far.

I should have come south from Hanover like a mouse with a cat in the room.

This wasn't very good and I sat in my sweat and watched them checking the papers. Situation: they stood about five yards from the car and they weren't looking at me and there was a flush of light rising from behind the long-hauler as someone else came homing in on the trap and in ten seconds or so they'd be dazzled by it if they looked in my direction so it wasn't a question of yards but of seconds and increasing candle-power.

The main police group was vetting the *Vollmond* truck in front of me, one of them climbing into the cab to have a look round: the theory they would be working on was that Martin might have thumbed a lift somewhere in the Linsdorf area after crashing the N.S.U. and might have offered the driver a fistful of deutschmarks to shove him under the seat if anyone turned nosey. The patrol with the lamp would be back there signalling the new arrival to halt: I could see his shadow stretching across the road-surface as the light brightened. Both trucks and the 17M had their engines switched off the newcomer was already producing a bit of background noise that would get louder until he stopped. No one would hear me open the door and I didn't have to slam it shut after me.

I turned my head and saw a couple of yards of empty road-margin and a line of thick brush. It was naked thorn but then they wouldn't like it either and its main value was visual: it would be like shooting through a smoke-screen.

A faint shrilling began and the shadow on the road was waving the lamp more insistently and I now had very little time to make the decision and my right hand was already reaching across to the other door because that was the way I'd be going out if I went out at all but the chances were about fifty-fifty. I knew I could get through the first of the thorn and break across open ground before they could draw and fire and the initial surprise phase would give me time to go a fair distance towards the next cover, but a loose shoe is more laming than a leg-wound and it would take up to three seconds to wrench both shoes off and a barefoot run across rough terrain would slow me critically.

And I would be committed.

The new arrival had stopped behind the long-hauler and the scene went dark. The last clear image on the retina was of the two uniformed men moving towards me, the senior holding my papers.

I took my hand away from the door. It had been mostly

stomach-think, not brain-think: the instinctive need of a trapped animal to free itself, the temptation to go as the hare had gone, ears flat and feet together. Brain-think had warned me. There had been a fifty-fifty chance of getting clear but my very freedom would have comprised another trap: I would have been committed, exposed as the man they were looking for. Martin. There was still a fifty-fifty chance of getting clear by sitting here with my nerves and sweating it out and if they finally let me drive away I would be uncommitted. Rödl.

'Good-morning.' A punctilious salute, the big hand swinging to touch the rock-like head, a hand that would come down with hammer-force if it sensed a wrong move.

'Good-morning,' I said.

'Where have you come from?' The robot tone of a speak-your-weight machine.

'Hanover.'

'Where are you going?'

'Münden.'

'Why are you on the road at this hour?'

'To avoid the traffic.'

I played it dead straight, not making a joke. Anyone trying to avoid the traffic and fetching up jammed between thirty tons' worth of truckage might think it rated a laugh but he wouldn't see it that way. Making a joke is fatal unless the worst thing on your mind is a duff rear-light because if they think you're not taking them seriously they'll have your shoes off and check them for hollow heels just to show how serious they can get.

It had gone very quiet now. Last man in had been told to switch off his engine. The *Hauptmann* was tapping my papers on the joint of his thumb. He said:

'What is the advantage of a hemispherical head?'

I looked a bit thrown, as if I hadn't quite caught on, because being too quick on the uptake can be as suspect as making a joke.

'Well, it cuts down turbulence, and if you've got twin overhead camshafts you'll want to incline the valves anyway so a hemispherical head's almost obligatory.'

'Have you any opinions on water-vapour?'

'In the carburation? I'd say it's a help in most conventional engines, in fact Schneider make a limited suction-feed system that anyone can fit. When my friends try to argue about this I always ask them why their car seems to run smoother on a wet day.'

The sweat was on my face now and I hoped he wouldn't notice. If he were going to keep me waiting five seconds before he spoke again it was going to be five seconds of purgatory, like waiting for the exam results. He wasn't only trying to find out if Karl Rödl, *Mechaniker*, knew his stuff on engines. He also wanted to test my German for mistakes in technical terms because any good linguist can come unstuck on words like camshaft. And the ice had been wafer-thin: the Striker wasn't internal-combustion and I hadn't needed this kind of terminology since the Nürburgring mission and the memory had had to pull it out of some very cold storage.

Visual accommodation was improving now and in the light of their torches I could see the group by the truck talking to the driver and his mate. One of them was still in the cab. The driver was shaking his head all the time – '*Nein, nein!*' The trouble with police traps is that even though they might be set up to intercept a man on the run they'll do what business is offered from an out-of-date licence to a crate of cocaine stowed under the seat and that means delay for everyone in the queue.

I didn't look up at the officer. I'd said my bit and now I was taking an interest in how the truck-driver was making out because he was being very emphatic about something and there was nothing else here to interest me.

'Very well.'

He handed my papers back. I turned my head after a second as if I'd just remembered them.

'Thank you.'

It wasn't the all-clear yet but the sweat began drying up. There were only two things left to worry about: they might ask for the car papers and they might ask me to get out. If they saw the car papers they'd want to know why I'd had to borrow the 17M in case it was because I'd had the bad luck to wreck an N.S.U. last night. And if I got out of the car I'd have to keep my bandaged hand and my split shoe out of sight and that wouldn't be too easy. It wasn't a black-and-white question of was I or was I not an Englishman named Martin. It was a question of watchful suspicion on their part, a trained eye open for minor irregularities, small inconsistencies, something not quite as it should be: a thread, however fine, that they could get between finger and thumb and pull and go on pulling till it thickened to a rope.

My chances were those of any candidate in an exam: they could ask the right questions (the ones I could answer) or the wrong ones (the ones I couldn't).

Light was spreading again. Someone else was closing on us from along the autobahn. I hardly noticed. I hardly noticed because the whole situation was presenting itself logically in my mind, perhaps as an antidote to fright. It went like this: Ferris would already be in signals with London and as long as the Bureau thought I was still of use they would move all available mountains to help get the Kriminalpolizei off my back. They had set me running and they wanted me to go on running in case by luck or acumen I found my way finally into what Parkis called the storm-centre. (There's an appalling amount of luck in the conduct of any mission however much acumen you try to bring it to: witness the collapse of Benedikt at a critical phase.) Of course the Bureau could do nothing officially: it didn't exist. But no network on a world scale is ever isolated: there's always a fringe overlap especially when something big is on the programme and any given agency will bump elbows with most organizations from the national civil police authorities up through the C.I.D. Special Branch, M.I.5., M.I.6. and the various select departments whose chiefs are known only to the P.M. and the Home Secretary. On an overseas mission you won't get far before you cross lines with the S.I.D., the C.I.A. or the Deuxième Bureau according to the area being worked. Interpol will often come into the picture because it has ninety-eight member-countries and that doesn't leave many places where they don't operate. (Interpol would at this moment see the name Martin coming up on their alert-programme because he was a British national in a foreign country and their main concern is with people crossing frontiers.)

Unofficially the Bureau would tap the odd grapevine here and there until they got a response from some organization they happened to have assisted at some time or other and if they could ease the right word through to Kriminalpolizei, Bundesrepublik Deutschland, a few telephones would ring and the heat would come off Martin even if he were being grilled in a cell on a murder charge.

But there was a limit to what action the Bureau could take and that limit was the line beyond which the Bureau would risk self-exposure. Of the sacred and unwritten laws that governed its constitution the most holy was that no one, however high, must in any circumstances, however grave, ever by word or deed or implication jeopardize the prime virtue by grace of which the Bureau was enabled to operate in areas and with resources outside the reach of other factions: the virtue of non-existence. Among the lower echelons where the ferrets ran we called it the Rule of the D.T.M.: otherwise *Don't Tell Mum*.

So the Bureau had a limit and so had I and it was the same one, the same precisely defined invisible line: because if these people asked to see the car papers or asked me to get out and open the luggage-boot and it led to a cell and a charge and a trial I would have to deal with it alone. From the moment of an official charge the Bureau would drop me like a dead rat. That was all right: it was in the contract. But my defence would already be spiked. To prove I hadn't killed Benedikt I would have to answer every question put by the prosecution and there'd be some I couldn't answer because it would mean crossing the line, exposing the Bureau.

When did you join the Accidents Investigation Branch of the Air Ministry, Herr Martin? What were you doing before then? Where did you train as an aviation psychologist? You can't answer? But surely you can tell us about your past? Your background? You'll be telling us next, Herr Martin, that you don't exist!

Correct.

They'd have it made. Acquaintance with the deceased – absence of alibi – fingerprints on the deceased's watch, lighter, pens – hasty departure from the motel – failure to complete accident report at hospital – acquisition of false papers – attempt to pass through police block under assumed identity. And finally the refusal to answer questions in court.

They don't hang you in West Germany these days. It would be a life sentence. But that wasn't the worst. Appeal. Tell them to look for the two men: the ones the manager saw with the deceased. If that was no use then I could stick it out till a chance came and I had a hacksaw blade and if the chance didn't come I could try to make a break from a working-party and if I couldn't make a break I could use a dinner-knife on the wrists and cut the rest of the sentence away. But all the time I was waiting for chances in there like a tethered goat I'd have to live with the thought that the Bureau was still running and the missions were still going out and there was one I hadn't finished. This one. That was the worst.

The flood of light grew brighter from behind and the shadow of the man with the signal-lamp moved sharply across the road. I tucked my papers away and looked up at the officer to see if that was all.

He said: 'Please open your luggage compartment.' He stood away from the door to give me room to get out.

Chapter Twelve

TO GROUND

The body of *Homo* is provided with various compensatory mechanisms. One is the carotid sinus, located in the neck.

'*Zu gross.*'

'*Sind Sie sicher?*'

When a man becomes angry the released adrenalin raises his blood-pressure throughout the system, putting incidental pressure on the carotid sinus. This triggers off a flow of nerve impulses to the brain which produce a calming effect in compensation. That is why the most heated anger cools the most quickly.

'*Probieren Sie diese an.*'

I put them on and walked round. They were unpolished stag-skin, high at the sides. The serration on the soles was only half-worn and they were dead quiet on the floor: that was important.

'*Ja, die passen.*'

The place was stuffed to the rafters with masculine accessories: shot-guns, fishing-rods, field-glasses, skis, windbreakers, boots and shoes. High in the gloom there was a diver's helmet. On his desk was a quarryman's detonator. It was a pity that I needed only shoes. You can do a lot with a quarryman's detonator.

'*Tragen Sie die gleich?*'

'*Ja.*'

They had buckles instead of laces and I took them up a notch. I was pleased with them, certainly not angry, but the carotid sinus works also in reverse. Low barometric pressure *outside* has the same effect as high blood-pressure *inside*. Since it can't tell the difference it sends the same nerve impulses to the brain, calming it down. Some people say: 'I'm sleepy, it must be the weather.'

He looked at my split shoe with a shrug.

'*Fertig.*'

'*Fertig.*' I nodded.

He dropped them both into an upturned fencing-mask and I gave him 60 DM, 20 for the shoes and 40 for the pair of ×6 Zeiss I had found on a shelf. He counted the deutschmarks in the light from the doorway. Over the Harz range the sky was a purple bruise. It was going to be a spectacular storm when it came, and this was why I felt sleepy.

Or it was the after-effects of the crash or the inadequate sleep at

Nitri's or the nervous tension of the police trap. Or I was getting old.

'*Auf Wiedersehen.*'

I went back to the car, walking normally for the first time since I'd left the motel. The left shoe felt too tight but it had two notches on each buckle the same as the other one: the foot had already tried to adapt itself to a split upper and now it would have to relearn.

'Certainly,' I had said, but it had been a nasty five minutes. The air was cold so I made a show of feeling the contrast, blowing out my cheeks as I left the car, one hand in my pocket for warmth, the other finding the right key as though it didn't have to think about it but it had to think about it bloody hard because it wasn't far from the driving-door to the boot and I was doing it one-handed and they were watching me and I knew that.

The latest arrival had doused his lights but it was still awkward having to keep one foot arched so that it sounded normal: it was trying to drag like a slipper. They both came with me, the young one holding the torch and aiming the beam at the boot-lock for me. It was the right key because there were three on the ring and the ignition and the door were the same pattern: one was a spare. But it didn't turn easily because the boot-lid was spring-tensioned by the rubber moulding and you normally had to press down a fraction with the left hand so the choice was to do it with the elbow and show I was injured or go on forcing the key till it snapped. If either happened it would finish me because they were looking for an injured man and if the key snapped they'd think I'd done it on purpose so that they couldn't look in the boot and see Walter Martin curled up there.

But there's a law of averages and my run of bad luck was stretching the odds a bit and the key turned and I raised the lid and they looked inside and that was that.

'Did you give anyone a lift at any time during the night?'

'No.'

'Did you see anyone thumbing you for a lift?'

'No.'

'Very well. You can proceed.'

Still very careful though, testing the lid to make sure it was properly locked, taking my time, there was no hurry. Because that's when they go on watching you in case you fall prone and give thanks to Allah for getting you off the hook. It still wasn't easy even then: the other group didn't like the way the truck-driver kept on saying '*Nein – nein!*' with so much emphasis and now they were helping him open the big double doors and the pig was laughing on both sides of its face. This meant I had to do a series of shunts between the two trucks before I could turn out and I had to do it one-handed, keeping the wheel locked over with my knee while I shifted the gears.

The young one swung his torch to guide me away and the officer saluted. The nerves began their reaction-phase and for the next kilometre I felt as if I'd drunk too much coffee.

None of the other shops were open yet: Münden is a small town and it was nearly full winter. I'd seen the old man swinging back his shutters and stopped on the off chance. It was probably his only life in there among the skis and divers' helmets: they were his toys.

The shoes were excellent and the left-foot clutchwork was normal again and I drove five kilometres without stopping while I worked out the situation and when I'd worked it out I turned into a minor road and found the right kind of spot and ran the 17M as deep as I could into a copse where raindrops still fell from the trees.

Situation: there might be just the two traps, one on each side of the Hanover–Kassel autobahn, or there might be a dozen, a quickly thrown net around Linsdorf. One of them was certain to be farther south towards Neueburg and I would hit in full daylight. No go. It would be safer to reach Neueburg by dark in any case: the guide book gave the population as under 5,000 so it was a place where a stranger would be suspect.

I set each window to an inch gap at the top and tilted the seat back and let sleep come.

Ferris had done a full coverage but there was nothing that he or Philpott or Dr Wagner or Nitri hadn't either told me or led me to consider.

List of witnesses. NB: These were sifted from several hundred and are believed to be the most reliable.

There were sixty-two names and full addresses. Farmers, postmen, bird-watchers, coastguard observers. Mostly farmers, like the one with the red tractor at Westheim. My own name wasn't among them: Ferris never joked on duty.

I just heard a whining noise, and looked up.

There weren't any flames as far as I could see, but the sun was partly in my eyes and shining on the wings, so I won't commit myself on that.

It was almost vertical and so close that I began to run. I remember thinking: 'Poor devil.' (I meant the pilot.)

The most common factor was the attitude.

Straight down. Vertical, or nearly vertical, I would say. He came down like a stone.

Chronologically there was no pattern. Thirty-six Strikers had crashed within three hundred and forty-two days. Average: one per 9.5 days. Longest interval between two crashes: 13 days. Shortest: 7.

Geographically there was no pattern. Out of ten main Striker bases each had experienced a crash: i.e., no squadron had been immune. Lowest incidence: 1. Highest: 5. (There was a slight tendency for high-incidence bases to appear in the north and Ferris hadn't missed it. *Frequency of accidents at Bederkesa, Quakenbrück, Oldenburg and Hankensbüttel is considered possibly due to weather conditions aggravating unknown effects. NB: Striker is sensitive to severe temperature change.*)

In the *Background of Dead Pilots* section there were several common factors but none were unexpected: each had a history with indications of what Dr Wagner called 'Striker psychosis' with attendant periods of anxiety states and hypertension. All had been sent once or more than once to Garmisch-Partenkirchen for two weeks' mud-baths and psychiatrical sessions. Confidential information on their private lives – so far as it could be obtained – showing nothing significant. Marital disturbance slight. Financial worries normal. Professional qualities well above average for front-line tactical squadrons – *NB: These pilots were picked from among all operational branches of the Luftwaffe in view of the technical sophistication and high cost of the Striker SK-6. They thus represent the élite of the German Air Arm.*

I went through the folder twice and used a pencil in the margins and filled the back cover with averages, common factors, consistencies, anomalies. Blank.

Some time during the afternoon I heard movement and kept perfectly still. I had slept from early morning till one o'clock and was ninety-eight per cent alert and two per cent under the continuing influence of the barometric pressure: the storm still sagged across the mountains, slow to break. The movement went on and sometimes the low leaves trembled within yards of the car. I saw him only once, crossing a clear patch: a wild boar, black, compact, full in tusk. and high at the shoulder. He swung his head and then stood rock-still, catching the unfamiliar smell of rubber and petrol, then vanished as if the leaves had drawn over him. He would have slept through the height of the day as I had, and would soon move through the night as I would, and I wished him well.

L-201 – *J*-136 – *S*-19. The identification figures were prefaced with a letter for each air base: Linsdorf – Jülich – Spalt. I went through the whole picture again and came up with nothing and put the folder away and took it out again on the spur of frustration.

Bederkesa – Quakenbrück – Jülich – Brüchsal ... North, North-west, West, South-west. It was consistent but this thing was full of consistencies and I was looking for anomalies, trying to see if the pattern broke anywhere. That might be a mistake.

Laubach – Linsdorf – Hankensbüttel – Oldenburg . . . East, North-east, North-east, North. It was consistent again and the pencil had made a ring on the map from North round the clock to North. I must have been over-concentrating because it was a minute before I got it. The names of the Striker bases made a geographical ring but I'd begun with a time-factor, not a space-factor. Ferris had called them pattern-crashes but he couldn't have known about this. In terms of *sequence* the Strikers had been crashing in a geographical ring round the map, North-West-South-East-North.

It practically spelled a name but I couldn't go back to Linsdorf: I was cut off from there and all I could do was file it.

I put the folder away.

Chapter Thirteen

THE FRONTIER

Neueburg was gnome-Gothic, a frontispiece for Grimm. The population must have been mostly pastoral because there weren't more than a hundred or so houses to the village. Pointed roofs, latticed windows, the glint of cats' eyes in doorways: even the weathervane over the pharmacy was a witch on a broomstick. Perhaps it was to mark her birthplace.

The early hunger of the day had passed off during the afternoon. It would return before midnight and I was tempted to pick up something to conserve but I didn't want to show my face anywhere. It would have to wait: in any case a light stomach would be an advantage if things got rough at the clockmaker's.

I didn't know. Benedikt hadn't told me whether the place were a safe-house for *Die Zelle*, a contact point of his own or a *Zelle* address where he was still accepted as loyal.

It was near the end of the main street. I assumed there was only one clockmaker's in Neueburg, otherwise Benedikt would have been more precise.

It backed on to a chapel so there wouldn't be a door at the rear. It made a corner of a T-section and if there were a second entrance it would be the door at the side, the first one along. I took the 17M past at normal speed and turned at the end of the village and came back, coasting to a stop just within observation-view of the front entrance and the door at the side. It was only ten minutes to five but the winter dark had already come down. The street-lamps were all right and I spent some time with the ×6 Zeiss after wiping the grime off the lenses.

In the next half an hour two people went in and came out. There was nothing about them to suggest they weren't fetching their alarm-clocks. I was in no hurry.

There are a few simple rules about visiting an indicated address and they add up to the one general idea of vetting the place carefully before going in. That was why I'd thought the Zeiss would be useful. After the first half an hour I had some data collected, mostly about the best way of getting out of the building if I found myself on the second or third floors and didn't want to use the front entrance. There were at least two people there because a light had gone on upstairs about fifteen seconds after someone had entered: there wasn't a lot of time to reach the third floor and the clockmaker would probably be talking to him in the shop itself.

Apart from general rules there were specific considerations. I might be recognised the instant I went in, either because they were in close touch with the *Zelle* unit in Hanover or because my face was probably now in the papers. There could be a dozen people in there – contacts, couriers, operators, radio-signallers – and I could walk straight into a spring-trap especially if Benedikt had talked before he died: if they knew he'd given me this address they'd expect me here.

General rules, specific considerations, instinct. The precise formula for doing the right thing in a given situation. But mostly instinct. The antennae weaving sensitively around and touching on hair-fine contacts, correcting and recorrecting the plan of approach, the conscious and sub-conscious gathering and relating of random data, computing, presenting, counselling telling me whether to cross over there and walk in now or wait another ten minutes or another sixty, whether to give the clockmaker Benedikt's name and assess his reaction or try one of a dozen other gambits that would leave us both with a way out if there were people there and it was dangerous.

Because I had to start with an assumption, a likelihood, as a blueprint. And I assumed that he was aware (1) that Benedikt had tried to defect and (2) that I knew it.

Normal data was coming in all the time and it could be vital or useless: seven cars driven through the village in half an hour, four of them Hanover-registered, two Frankfurt and one Stuttgart. A light-coloured Porsche had pulled up fifty yards ahead of the 17M and a man had gone into the shop and driven off again after five minutes. Thirteen people had passed me on foot and ten had gone by the clockmaker's, four of them looking in, one of them giving a wave of his hand. Two had gone in and come out again.

An Opel Kapitän stopped a short way down the side-street and a man got out and went into the first doorway along. I'd had the Zeiss on him and so I was certain. I supposed he had come south as I had, perhaps going to ground as I had, and for the same reason: to wait for the police traps to be withdrawn. The manager of the motel would have described him to the Kriminalpolizei and he would know that. In the ordinary way it might not worry him: a verbal description isn't much to go on. So I assumed it had been important for him to reach Neueburg and the doorway over there in complete security. The death of Benedikt could have sent the entire network quivering and its controllers would be jumpy.

He had left the Kapitän a few yards from the door and had walked along to it lightly on the balls of his feet, his shoulders forward. I didn't need to go across and put my head inside the car to confirm what I already knew would be there: a faint smell of almonds.

He was in the house for an hour and during that time I twice decided to make a move and follow him through the side door and take it from there on an *ad hoc* basis and twice revoked the decision and tried to sell myself the idea that it wasn't because my left hand didn't want to get hurt any more.

There were in fact practical reasons why I should avoid immediate risks. Up to an hour ago I'd had only one fine thread to follow: the name of a village where there was a clockmaker. If that information had turned out to be duff or if I'd made a mistake at the autobahn police trap my personal part in the mission would have been totally written off. Without this one fine thread there would have been no future: I was isolated now, cut off from Linsdorf and the ability to root around there under the A.I.B. cover. And there was nowhere else to go. It would have been the first time I had ever failed to report back to the Bureau without at least some bits and pieces for them to look at.

But now I had something for Ferris: the location of a *Zelle* safe-house, confirmed. If I went in there the chances of learning a lot more were high but the chances of bringing the information away with me were not. If I stayed where I was I'd be sitting pretty and I didn't want to jog the barber's arm.

One factor made the final decision. It was a factor that often influences an operation at any given critical stage and it is surprising because it is banal: it is the weather. Tonight over Neueburg the sky was still clear, with the storm-clouds piled and concentrated in the Harz range to the north. A haze was spreading eastwards from the centre but the third-phase moon was still at nine-tenths luminosity and its light would last until the storm broke. Without it I would have had to go in there and do what I could because there would have been no alternative.

He came out alone and went straight to the Kapitän without checking the street and if Ferris ever saw one of us do a thing like that he'd have us underneath the Lowry for filthy rotten security. Perhaps that's why the Bureau had lasted so long.

I gave him fifty seconds and started up and tagged him out of the village at long range, settling down at something like a hundred yards through the hedgerows south. I didn't expect it to be easy but it was worse than I'd let myself believe. Across flatter terrain the going would have been comfortable because his rear-lamps and the light thrown by his heads would have provided a continuous beacon for me but in this area the rise and fall of the road blotted him out at intervals and I had to use the moon alone. After the first few kilometres I could feel the ciliary muscles contracting and relaxing as my eyes adjusted to the changing light-conditions. That was all right: they could go on doing it and the exercise was good for them but the roads were narrow and there was often a temptation to flick the heads on for half a second to make sure I wasn't going to hit anything. Even the sidelamps would have been a help but from the moment I switched them on he'd pick me up in the mirror and start watching me and wait for me to turn them off somewhere and I wasn't going to do that.

Nervous hallucinations set in after thirty minutes or so. They were bound to. When he topped a brow and vanished beyond it his image remained on the retinae and when he reappeared before it had time to fade out I could see two of him because he never showed up exactly in the same place on the vision-field. He wasn't going fast but it was too fast to take an accurate line through the bends and I clouted a bank before long and had to fight off the subsequent yawing-action that was set up by the springs.

Trees were the biggest hazard: they hid him suddenly if the road dipped or turned at that point and as soon as my eyes adjusted to the moonlight I was running into the trees myself and the whole lot went dark because they hid the sky as well and I was driving blind for five-second periods at sixty k.p.h. and at that speed I was covering more than eighty metres blacked out.

The only time for thinking was along the stretches of straight road where I slowed a fraction to increase the gap and make it more difficult for him to pick up reflected light in his mirror. There were no facts to go on except that since he'd turned south from Neueburg he wasn't heading for Hanover where he was probably based and this gave me a chance to get some more information provided I could stay with him to the end of the line. There were a few assumptions, one of them reasonable: the clockmaker's must be a safe-house or a radio-point or both, but nothing more: an organization capable of half crippling the Luftwaffe's front-line strike-force and removing the Army Chief-of-Staff and the Minister of the Interior from office wouldn't make its headquarters in Neueburg. Another assumption – possibly more wishful than reasoned – was that the man ahead of me was making direct for those headquarters either in the routine duty of courier or to report on Benedikt. One thing was certain: I had to go with him.

We were thirty-one kilometres south of Neueburg on the speedo-trip when his lights vanished and I drove by the moon until some trees came and the offside of the 17M ploughed clay from the bank and struck roots and began creasing: the weight was shifting and the front tyre howled like a buzz-saw as the wing folded against it and I tried to ease over without correcting too sharply and hitting the opposite bank. Thorn and the boughs of saplings whiplashed along the bodywork and there was a dead-weight feeling to the wheel so I gunned up and dragged her clear and hit the lights on because there was the chance he wouldn't see them whereas there was no chance of dodging a head-on impact if the whole thing ran wild: without his lights and without the moon I was driving into a waste of darkness and the margin of error was the width of the car subtracted from the width of the road and it wasn't enough to get me through.

The whole scene jumped into focus as the lights came on: road-surface and grass and earth banks and a gateway and a group of elms rearing with the interplay of light and shadow swinging through their columns. It began from there: a series of rocking lunges that took the car through a zig-zag from bank to bank with the nearside rear skinning bark from an elm and the springs pitching so hard that the steering was half under control and half abandoned as the front wheels slid and struck earth and bounced away and found a grip and lost it again. Given some calculated bursts of acceleration the trim would have steadied but I was having to slow, having to brake because it was the only chance.

There were three more impacts at acute angles before I could pull up with all four wheels in a slide. As soon as movement stopped I cut the lights and hit the door open. I was in a hurry now and the wing came clear of the front tyre because it had to, because I made it, the left hand hooking to help, the bandage catching on the torn edge of the metal, some of it tearing. Then I stood and listened, seeing a patch of light flickering a kilometre away, south and eastwards.

He'd taken a branch road and that was why he'd been hidden for so long. He couldn't have seen my lights or heard the wing on the tyre because he would have stopped and doused his own lights and lain low. So there was still a chance.

It took time to come up on him again. The land was flatter, eastwards, but twice I had to light up for other traffic and once I lost him for minutes through a region of brush. Petrol fumes were filling the interior, and backdraught bringing them in through gaps in the torn bodywork: the tank had been split at some time when the rear had struck obstacles. It was a new worry but there was nothing I could do about it except coast when there was a chance, conserving fuel.

The moon was the only reference for any kind of bearing and I estimated that we were only some forty kilometres east of our north-south leg from Neueburg to the point where he'd turned off. I didn't know the area but I had looked at the map Ferris had put into the statistics folder and when the Kapitän slowed and turned across rough ground and doused its light I knew that this could only be the East German Frontier Zone.

It was a winter silence. The moon's light blanched colour away and left a bone-white landscape. There was no frost but the air was cold and very still. Far north the first murmuring came from the cloud-mass but here the land was quiet.

He had run the car into a huddle of black oblongs: the hulk of a military depot left here to rot a quarter of a century ago. When he had turned off the road I had started coasting with the engine dead, letting the last of the momentum thrust the 17M into thick bush. I pushed the statistics folder under the carpet and got out.

111

For a minute the black outline was unbroken, then he detached himself and began walking. I drew my left hand along one of the wheel-ruts where the earth was soft at the edges, darkening the bandage, then took up the tag. I think he looked round but no more than casually and I was motionless before his eyes could have focussed. A light flickered as he checked his watch and I knew there was a rendezvous.

We walked fifty-odd metres apart. I was ready at every pace to freeze if he looked back. He didn't look back.

Between the North Sea and Czechoslovakia runs the jagged scar of the Frontier, nine hundred miles of barbed wire, trenches, watchtowers, concrete bunkers and minefields. For West Germany it doesn't exist: East Germany doesn't exist, therefore it can possess no frontier. But it is there, manned by fourteen thousand troops of the Deutsche Demokratische Republik with machine-guns, searchlights and dog-patrols. In the sensitive areas where attempts at 'exfiltration' are insistent the vigilance is sharp and every day someone, somewhere along the nine hundred miles of the Frontier, dies, a worn coat puckered by a bullet and a hand going out to break the fall of the living body that is dead before it meets the ground; and there is special leave for the man who shot him down.

The Hanover section is the responsibility of the Federal Customs and is patrolled by the Bundesgrenzschutz and the British Frontier Service. It is a less sensitive area and reliance is placed on the barbed wire and mines. It is not the only section where vigilance on the part of the East German Volkspolizei has become cursory: since the Frontier was fortified in 1961 more than two thousand of their own border troops have themselves crossed it from east to west.

In some places the wire has rusted and the loose boards of the watchtowers rattle in the wind; the warning signs lean from rotten posts and the patrols keep to the warmth of their huts unless a sound reaches them through the winter night. But the mines are there, sown invisibly across the thirty-metre strip of desolate land. Some people still get across. There is a match-seller who sits outside the Hauptbahnhof in the city of Hanover, legless.

South and east from Neueburg are pine forests, the haunt of wild boar, but a lot of timber has been cut and the land ploughed: in many places the horizon is low and distant across a waste of beet-fields. The wind has an edge when it blows from the north and there is not much shelter.

It was here that he led me, the man who liked marzipan.

112

A notice leaned in the moonlight, propped on the barbed wire. *Halt! Hier Zonengrenze. Achtung! Lebensgefahr: Wirkungsbereich Sowjetzonaler Minen. Halt!*

Following him I had looked back a dozen times, sighting on the ruin of the military depot and keeping in line with it so that if he turned his head I would be seen against its shape and thus perhaps not seen at all. Also I noted landmarks: a hump of withered bush, the skeleton form of a watchtower to my left, the ash-grey shape of what looked like a concrete bunker on the other side.

He went straight through the wire and I stood watching him, keeping quite still because as he stooped to pass between the strands the pallor of his face showed up. But he didn't expect to be followed: his head was turning to left and right and I saw a new shape, smaller than the bunker and farther away and with a vertical blade of light cutting its mass. It would be a guard-hut, the light showing through the join of a door. He checked it and then went on but more slowly because the sign had said *Danger of Death*.

I waited. He had stopped and stood motionless but I heard no sound anywhere. Then he began going forward again at an angle and I walked to the wire and went through it as he had. The barbs had been turned inwards with pliers along a metre of its length and as I straightened up I took another bearing and committed it to memory.

He had stopped again and his head was turning and I stood waiting. The white of his face was showing now and he had swung his body in my direction and for half a minute he made no movement at all. I wasn't sure that he had seen me. It was an eerie place, a landscape with dead figures: the posts leaning like gibbets and the web of the wire breaking the flat two-dimensional background into sections as if the whole scene were cardboard, a badly lighted stage. Perhaps it was difficult for him to believe in the unlikely: that a man was standing not far from him, thrown up from the waste of earth where armies had once passed, leaving their dead. Perhaps he was afraid of his own imaginings and even hoped it was in fact a man of flesh and blood that stood here, a creature he could deal with, natural, mortal.

Neither of us could move easily, move quickly, here. They were lying quietly, the brass-capped detonators, an inch below the surface of the earth, protected by their pitch-mouldings against the rain. He knew where they were but it was only another way of saying that he knew he mustn't move too quickly, here.

Then I was sure that he had seen me, recognized me at least for something that shouldn't be here, something that was neither a post nor a shadow thrown by the moon. His outline was changing slowly on one side and now the pale light flickered on metal in his hand.

Softly: 'Who is there?'

Chapter Fourteen

STORM-CENTRE

I went up to him slowly, following the angle he had taken. The earth was crusty with frost.

'You can't use that,' I said. 'It'd make too much noise.'

He held it cocked up to aim at my face. It was his usual, the P38, and he remembered what he'd been taught: at close quarters it has to be the heart or the brain because anywhere else is too slow and even two or three in the stomach won't stop you from trying to take a man with you bare-handed if your blood's up. And you might have anything under a thick sheepskin coat: wallet, holster, so forth.

Sweat was on his face, a grey dew in the moonlight. His breathing was shaky and it confirmed what I'd felt about him two nights ago when he'd sat behind me in the 250 SE with this thing lined up with the bridge of my nose: he was gun-dependent.

'Don't move,' he breathed.

'Go on, then, get it over.' I was suddenly fed up because we were wasting time. 'Then see how far you'll get before they're out of that hut. They've got the real thing, rapid-fire.'

'*Don't speak so loud.*' Soft panic on his breath. He'd crossed here before but he didn't like it.

'That's what I mean.' I'd been getting it ready over a period of several seconds, working out the exact way it would have to go, and the gun smashed upwards into his face and didn't go off because the blow was directly on the wrist-nerve to paralyse the fingers before the index could contract but there was risk attached and I had to sweat it out until the gun hit the ground with a negative thud and didn't blow our legs off.

He was worse then I'd thought, even though I knew what they were like, the gun-dependents: take their toy away and they break down blubbing. He just rocked stupidly with a hand up to his face and didn't do anything about me at all so I cancelled the second half of the trick – the knee-to-groin number – and picked up the P38 and threw it well across the wire where it would be all right.

'You go first,' I said.

Reaction was setting in and I wasn't feeling much better than he was: it had been a rough run from Neueburg in the dark and it had looked so many times as if the best I could hope to do was climb out of a smashed 17M just as I'd climbed out of a smashed N.S.U. and at every one of those times the whole mission had depended on which way a one-ton mass would swing when it left my hands.

Now I could relax.

'There are mines here,' he said. His mouth had begun bleeding.

'I can read.'

'You'll have to go back.'

It was just because he didn't know what to do. A lot of them are like that: they work to strict orders and when there aren't any orders they beat the air. But I knew it would be all right: I had known since he'd looked at his watch just after he'd left the car. He had a rendezvous.

'You go first,' I told him. 'And start now. They're not going to wait for ever.'

He was staring into my face, intent on everything I said, hoping it might give him some kind of direction: and finally it did. He had needed telling almost in so many words that all he had to do was take me with him to the rendezvous where 'they' were waiting. Then he could ask one of them for a gun and he would be six feet tall again and I would be dead.

'It is heavily mined,' he said slowly. 'You will have to take care.'

A new thought had been worming its way through the sludge: he was worried in case I trod on the wrong thing and brought the guards out firing from the hip. He only liked shooting people: he didn't like people shooting him.

'We'll both be very careful, yes. Both of us.'

He nodded and turned away and went forward for three or four metres at a time, stopping to check bearings. There was something disgusting about the way I had to put my feet precisely where he put his, turning my head exactly as he did: it was just deep in my nature to resent being dependent on people, even people as good as Ferris, and now I was dependent on this gross creature, my life linked intimately with his.

He moved again and stopped again and I checked the new reference: the third wire-stanchion from the nearest warning-sign was lined up with the edge of the ruin. I assumed we were halfway across the thirty-metre strip because he began checking ahead for bearings instead of behind. It was easier in that direction: pines stood sparsely at the fringe of a darker mass and the intervals between their trunks were irregular so that each had identity.

The lightning flashed and everything leapt sharply in it: trees, wire, posts, the rutted earth. He caught his breath and stumbled. The pathology of the gun-dependent is odd: once armed he loses his fear even of things against which a gun is of no use: spiders, heights, the elements. He carries a magic talisman. Conversely, deprived, his fears are exaggerated.

The lightning struck twice again and flickered out and for a moment it was difficult to see. We had both stopped. The Harz range stood fifty or sixty kilometres to the north but the storm had been drifting south-east and the thunder reached us in less than one minute. I looked up and saw that the moon was now ten or twelve degrees of arc from the edge of the cloud-mass.

I said: 'We haven't got long.'

He moved again, counting seven paces and checking. The post was lined up with the fourth pine from the end but I used one of the wire-stanchions as the closer reference because it was thinner and therefore more accurate. He was taking his time and I began thinking it had been a mistake to throw the bloody thing away: his confidence had gone with it.

'Look, we've got about nine minutes' visibility left so for God's sake get off the pot.'

Through his teeth: 'You want me to blow myself up?'

'If it'll get you off the pot.'

Halfway to the eastern wire my weight broke the crusty earth and one shoe slipped on the shoulder of something hard. I said: 'Wait.'

I made sure he stopped, then bent down and felt the thing because I needed to know how good his bearings were. The soil came away under my fingers and I went on clearing it until they could define the shape. It was a curved shoulder and pitch-smooth and the detonator would be three or four inches to the right, in the centre. It would be at least a fourteen-ounce actuator, otherwise the odd crow or some heavy rainfall would trip it, so I finished the job and left the whole thing exposed: it would be a help if I ever came back this way and if I didn't it would help someone else.

'You're not very good,' I said, 'are you?'

It was just possible that he'd deliberately taken me too close but I didn't think so: even in his demoralized condition he must realize that he'd catch some of the blast.

'You shouldn't have done that.' His whisper was reedy with fright.

'You shouldn't have taken me so bloody close.'

There were two more changes of angle before we reached the wire and I took a final sighting with the military depot as a reference. It looked closer than I would have believed: the nerves had come farther than thirty metres. He climbed through the wire, more confidence in his movements now that we were clear of the mines and he could lead me to his friends and borrow a gun. When he'd gone five paces I said sharply:

'What was that?'

He turned his head and I did it and when he was down I looked for his papers. All he had were an identity card and a crossword puzzle and I held my watch-glass at an angle against the name to increase the light-factor. Gühl. Re-check, Gühl. I kicked a hole in the earth and buried the card and put the crossword puzzle into my coat as a flash came. There were three more over a ten-second period and I kept still until they were over. He lay in much the same position as Benedikt but there were no bits of porcelain around, just the scuffed earth.

I had waited until he had taken his last five paces so as to know the direction of the rendezvous. It lay towards the group of pines and I started off. The sound of the preliminary flash was already crackling and the rest of the series followed and sent a ricochet of echoes from the Thüringerwald range to the south-east so that for longer than half a minute the sky and earth reverberated.

The dark came down soon afterwards, sweeping from west to east across the land as the clouds reached and drew beneath the moon. I should have made him push on faster through the mines instead of wet-nursing him: the rendezvous could be a kilometre from here and if I missed it the one fine thread would break. Or I should have let him take me further than those five paces but the trouble was that I couldn't stand his company.

A long flash broke, a chain-discharge that went rippling across the dark mass of the trees and dusted them with grey-green light. I froze and waited, uneasy now because this was a patch of open ground where there was nothing higher than a clod of earth and anyone could pick me off with the other hand behind their back. The thunder arrived within a few seconds: at ground level the air was calm but a high wind-layer was shifting the storm-clouds at increasing speed. Then light flashed once and I wasn't ready for it because it didn't come from the sky. It could have been the nerves:

I was stumbling blind across furrows and the spine was taking some of the shocks. The trunk of the first pine loomed and I began crossing the gap to the next one.

'*Hier.*'

I had overshot quite a bit and had to turn back and to the left before I saw it. There was still ploughed earth underfoot so they must have brought it right to the dead-end of the track.

I got in and said: 'You'd better get away quite fast because I kicked up some noise coming across.' The dash-lamp threw a weird greenish glow on the driver's face. He had his neck screwed round to look at me and I stared back at him. 'What the hell did you have to flash your light for?' I said. 'Did you think I couldn't find you or something?' He didn't move but his eyes switched twelve inches to my left.

She asked from beside me: 'Where is he?'

'Gühl? Crossing tomorrow night. You'll have to meet him.' Her one question had been clipped and authoritative so I said: 'Just tell him to shove off, will you? There's two of them out there looking for the noise I made.'

She told him: 'Wait for the next thunder.'

'*Kamerad Oberst.*' He faced the front.

'What happed to Gühl?'

Lightning flared and I was looking into bronze eyes, their brilliance heightened by the flash: then it was over but I had seen her face, hard, proud, altered by the storm and my strangeness.

'I was ordered across first.' The thunder shook the night and the engine started up and we were on the move before the echoes died away. 'You want an intelligent report, don't you? You think *he* knows what the hell's going on? He's a clod, you know that.'

The track gave on to a metalled road within a hundred metres and we stopped bumping around.

'How did you injure yourself?'

She didn't miss much: he hadn't switched the heads on yet and there was no back-glare. She'd taken me all in, just in the one flash.

'The nail-file slipped.' We got into higher gear and now he switched them on so I hunched myself round a bit more to face her. Night-black hair, close-cropped but not masculine, pale lipstick, if any, a lean hard jaw-line, the nose by Michelangelo. 'What do you imagine things are like in Hanover with the Benedikt thing just blown up? I was lucky to get off with a stray one in the hand.' It was the sort of face you'd expect to see at a night-rendezvous in the East German Frontier Zone if you expected to see a woman there at all. 'Anyway,' I said wearily, 'we've stopped the leak, that's the main thing.'

She kept her hands inside her battered flying-jacket. Perhaps she had a gun but I didn't think so: one sharp word to the Prussian-headed type at the wheel and he'd swing one on me without even swerving. He'd called her *Oberst*: Colonel. She asked:

'How far had it gone?'

'What?'

'The leak.'

'*Christ*, don't you know *anything*? Didn't Neueburg keep you informed?'

She didn't answer but I wasn't worried. You don't set up a contact point thirty kilometres from a frontier without putting radio in. I let the silence go on for a bit and then said: 'I'll tell you how far it had gone. He'd made contact – *twice*. We got the one in Hanover and he went and did it again: he knew how to try, I'll give him that much.' The scene was lit up around us and I had to shout against the din. 'It was Gühl who was sent in to fix him the second time, at Linsdorf. I thought they were *your* orders through Hanover. If they weren't yours then whose were they for God's sake?'

She might have answered me, given me a name, a hand-hold, but there was a flash so bright that it looked as if the whole sky had fused: the headlights seemed to go out and the entire landscape went lichen-green and the thunder rolled between the hills with one long-drawn-out bowling-alley clatter. It was appropriate enough: I was on my way to what London called the 'storm-centre' and bloody Parkis was right again.

The last lot had been tough on the ear-drums because when it was quiet again I could barely hear the engine. It was a three-cylinder Wartburg 1000, a home-product they described as a 'limousine' along the Unter den Linden though along Oxford Street it'd be a clapped-out minicab.

'Where did they call you from?'

She had a low and rather husky voice, the kind people wish they could keep once their cold has gone. It would have been attractive if every time she spoke I didn't expect her to tell the Prussian to pull up and get in the back with us and bring his garotting tools.

'Berlin.'

'When?'

'Too late, as usual. No bloody co-ordination.' I said in sudden frustration: 'You know the trouble with *Die Zelle?* It's over-organized. Its left hand's so busy trying to find out what its right hand's doing that it can't even feel the way along the wall.' I looked for reaction but she just watched me, chin resting on the fleece collar of the jacket, saying nothing either with her eyes or her mouth. 'Look at the Hanover cell: they didn't get on to Benedikt till it was damned nearly too late. And who did the job on Stöckener? They weren't too clever, getting him *alone* in his car before they shoved it off the road – made it twice as difficult and in the end it stank of foul play. What's one West German military driver among friends? Who went soft?'

I looked away from her and left it at that. A lot of it didn't add up but that was all right: I'd been called in late so I wouldn't be expected to know some of the answers. I just wanted to show I at least knew some of the questions.

It was a long time before she spoke. We passed one of the Soviet garrison barracks, a litter of two-storey hutments behind a picket fence with machine-gun towers. This side of the frontier there were twenty Russian divisions and they'd been here twenty years.

'Did you talk to Benedikt?'

'Of course I talked to him. Poor bastard, he was too good for this world, you know that?'

Lightning came again but this time there was quite an interval before the thunder followed. When the greenish glow brightened again on the facia-board I took another sighting on the speedo-trip. We'd gone twenty-seven kilometres from the frontier, due east most of the time, and it couldn't be far now because the fuel was below a quarter and there wouldn't be a filling-station open at night: we'd seen only two cars since we'd got on to the wider roads south of Mülhausen and there wasn't even an oil-streak along the nearside lane. In the Deutsche Demokratische Republik if you weren't military or political you walked.

'Who was your controller in Hanover?'

'I never even saw him. They shot me straight in to locate Benedikt and stop the rot.' I'd rehearsed it so many times that it seemed to make sense. There were half a dozen other direct questions I'd rehearsed the answer to but now she threw one in that I couldn't hope to stop.

'Who was your controller in Berlin?'

Because you might get away with not knowing the people you've been sent in to assist but if you don't know the name of your own controller at your own base there's something just a fraction odd in the picture.

I hitched myself round and looked at her and waited until she turned her head and then I said: 'Look, I think you're old enough to know. I haven't been in East Germany since the night in 1945 when I was holed up for six hours in the undercarriage of a converted bomber that was due out of Leipzig with a cargo of antityphoid serum for Berlin. Maybe you know how long I've been working for *Die Zelle* on the other side of the frontier and if you don't it doesn't matter but I'll tell you this: you may be one of the hierarchy at HQ and I could trust you with my last wristwatch but the dreary fact of the matter is that until tonight I didn't know your face and I still don't know your name, *Kamerad Oberst*, so if it's all the same to you I'm going to play it a bit coy when you throw questions like that one. Because if *you* don't know who my controller is in Berlin I might be a fool to tell you.' There were gold flecks deep in the bronze but that was all, just the play of light on living colour. 'No offence, of course.'

When the eyes of two people meet and hold their gaze a silent conversation begins and when they are strangers there is a great deal to be said because their lives are a blank to each other. But sometimes there is even more to be withheld and nothing of it must show and for some people it is difficult. For the woman sitting close to me in the Wartburg, her face sometimes shadowed and sometimes lit by the storm, it was easy. She had spent her life withholding things which spoken, even by the eyes, could betray her: she was a professional, the kind you occasionally meet in the bitter and grinding course of a mission and wish you could perhaps have met in some better place and at some better time when life held more promise of being longer. So that there was nothing in these honeyed tiger's eyes at all. And nothing, as I knew, in my own.

'We shall be there soon,' she said and looked away.

The moon was behind cloud and the land dark. From the distance the building made a honeycomb pattern of light as if a liner were moored there on still black water.

Three men at the gates checked us in. One carried a repeater rifle but wore no uniform: I knew his type, the blank face, the attitude half-slack, half-military, the air of unlimited power subordinate only to higher-ranking members of the same régime – the secret police.

'*Kamerad Oberst*.' The click of heels.

All I could see of the building was that it was modern, a slab of raw concrete with the silhouette of shiplamps jutting on the skyline. Most of the windows were barred and I heard dogs somewhere. The certainty was satisfying: the thread had held and now I had come all the way. This was the storm-centre: the *Kommandantur* of *Die Zelle*.

Two plain-clothes guards fell in as we climbed the steps but she dismissed them with a word and we went into the building alone. Two others met us and she sent for someone by name and we stood in a silent group until he appeared, a complex of hooded spotlights casting our shadows across the floor.

She didn't look at me: her head was turned away. Standing, she was a slight figure even in the flying-jacket though taller than I had imagined. She stood easily erect, gloved hands behind her.

'*Kamerad Oberst?*'

A big man, quiet on his feet, his eyes dulled by the long absence of any need to think.

Her neat head turned to look at him.

'This man crossed tonight. His name is Martin. Take him to Reception and search him. Strip him and search his body. Search the bandage particularly. Make certain there is no death-pill anywhere on him. Let him dress and then restrict his movements. If he should kill himself before the *Herr Direktor* can interrogate him I shall hold you responsible.'

She left us without looking back.

Chapter Fifteen

KÖHN

The passages were as wide as in any modern building in East Germany and there were no other guards within sight but the place had the atmosphere of a penitentiary.

'Is this a school?'

When they have dull eyes don't ask them what something is: they won't tell you. Give them a bone: the pleasure of correcting you.

'This is the Aschau Asylum for the Criminally Insane.'

The room where they took me seemed appropriate. The big man went in first and the other followed me. Iron bed, metal handbasin, spotlights in a low ceiling: there were a lot of these lights about the place, all the better to see you with. One window, adequately barred, a quarter-inch-steel door with a continental double-action lock and a sliding grille-panel where they could look in to see what you were doing.

The escort stayed in the doorway and the big man became a mechanical valet. She had said do this, do that, and now he did this, did that. The instructions had gone into his skull and the actions came out through his hands: he searched me and stripped me and searched my body and searched the bandage particularly and made sure there was no death-pill on me, then he let me dress and restricted my movements with a pair of military handcuffs, arms behind, because you can get through a vein with your nails if you work at it and she'd warned him that he was responsible for me. The other man stood near the door bouncing gently on his arches like a boxer fresh into the ring, the night-stick looped to his wrist with a leather thong.

The bandage was difficult because some of the stitches had pulled – probably when I'd tugged the edge of the wing clear of the tyre – and the blood had congealed, but we managed it in the end. The other one, right fore-arm, was perfectly clean. His dull eyes wandered over me and he kept turning me round and lifting my arms, a Simian frown of puzzlement forming slowly across his brow. It would take time for someone like this to catch up with progress and I assumed he was wondering why there weren't any bits of Elastoplast here and there because in the old days it used to be all the rage: you could pack a 1000-x microfilm and a flat-mould cyanide dose under quite a small strip and still leave room for the handbook.

They went away. They took the obvious things with them: sheepskin coat, papers for Walter Martin, papers for Karl Rödl, Striker statistics folder, crossword puzzle. I was worried about that: even in the moonlight it had looked very like a plan of the minefield layout Gühl had kept on him in case he wanted to check his bearings. They had taken the coat because it was so thick – you could secrete photostat copies in triplicate of the entire Early Warning System from Mexico to Nova Scotia in a coat like that – and because Nitri had patched it so neatly and they wanted to know why. They had taken the arm-sling I'd been given at the hospital because it would be possible for me to hang myself with it but they had left Nitri's scarf because it wouldn't.

I had only just finished checking the door-lock and the window-bars when they fetched me out and took me along to a small surgical ward where a doctor redressed my hand. He was a civilized man and asked if there were anything I wanted so I said food. They took me back to 'Reception' and after fifteen minutes a heavy-breasted girl in brogues brought a tray and left it with me. The big man unlocked the handcuffs and took them away with him. It must have been on orders: he would never have worked it out for himself that no one can eat with his hands behind his back.

No knife, no fork, nothing for surprise attack or self-infliction I hadn't expected to be given. I hadn't expected to be given caviar either but there was a fair-sized paper picnic plate full of the stuff, spread for me on strips of buttered toast as neatly as you'd spread rat-poison. Beer in a soft plastic cup.

It had to be a brain-think all the way because my last meal had been with Benedikt the night before and I was already salivating. (1) If they wanted to kill me they could do it more cheaply than this way. (2) If they wanted me unconscious the same applied. (3) I hadn't been interrogated yet and they wouldn't learn much if I had to be carried to the grilling-room insensible or dead. (4) There was no effective drug in the oral-administration group that would force me to reveal what I didn't want to reveal.

Provided the foregoing were acceptable the fifth consideration was decisive: this stuff was high in protein, fats and carbohydrates. No value in the salt content but enough sugar in the beer to feed the muscles for a limited period.

I ate slowly.

They had taken away my watch to have it probed but by estimation it was an hour later when they came for me again.

That would make it approximately midnight. I had been keeping a conscious check on the passage of time since the watch was taken: it wouldn't be important for a while but I didn't know how things would go here and it might later be useful, even vital, to judge the coming of daylight.

They were the same two and they took me down to the main hall. It seemed busy, so late, but some of the spotlights were out and people talked quietly. Three men were passing through the hall, dark-suited and preoccupied, the members of a consultant body convening to discuss a recent autopsy. It was what they looked like but they might have been anyone: anyone important. My escort stopped them and spoke to the one with the rebuilt face and he glanced at me and nodded and went on with his colleagues.

'We will wait,' the big man said. He looked as if he'd waited all his life at some bus-stop where the road was closed. Other people went through, some of them women with patient faces that looked at nobody else: Vidauban is very good at this, with his interiors grey-toned and peopled with dream figures that however crowded appear uninvolved with each other.

From somewhere higher in the building a sound reached us and

I didn't want to think it was a human voice because a human voice ought not to sound like that.

Quick footsteps and an interchange of words. The big man said tonelessly: 'We will go to the office of the *Herr Direktor* now.'

It was a long room with a low acoustic ceiling and an internal-communications complex on a desk. Black chairs with the East German equivalent of PVC upholstery and chrome legs, an ebonite console on one wall with some of the panels illuminated. From here they could probably diagnose a schizophrenic crisis in Patient 99, Cell 104, South Block, and prescribe shock-treatment.

They were the same three men but two of them said nothing and did nothing all the time I was there. The one who spoke to me was the one with the rebuilt face.

'Sit down, Herr Martin.'

There was a spare chair but no one else came. He sat behind the desk. Above him on the wall was the expected portrait of Walter Adolphovich Ulbricht, First Secretary of the Sozialistische Einheitspartei Deutschlands.

'I will call you Martin because that is the name we have known you by –' he put the two identity cards together and pushed them aside – 'since you arrived in Hanover from London.'

I had never seen him before tonight but I recognized him now. With only the face to go on it would gave been difficult. The left eye was artificial but a perfect match and I wouldn't have suspected it if the original injury had been less massive: the face on that side couldn't have been damaged to that extent without the eye going too. The rebuilding had been beautifully done: the surgeon was a portrait artist and it was the very excellence of his technique that showed the change. One side of this man's face had continued to age and the new side was still young: Dorian Gray and his portrait all in one.

'Do you know where you are?'

'I've got a rough idea.'

You don't have secret police guarding the gates of an asylum for the criminally insane and you don't send a secret police colonel to pick up couriers at the Frontier and bring them here if your sole business is to look after manic depressives.

'This is Aschau.' He wasn't interested in my rough ideas. 'Have you heard of it?'

'Yes.'

'Where?' Rather quickly.

'The big slob mentioned it.'

One of the committee moved his head and I got the feeling that people weren't meant to talk like that to the *Herr Direktor*.

He didn't seem to mind. When you've caught a winged pigeon you must expect the odd drop of lime on your hand while you examine it. (It wasn't because Aschau was meant to be an asylum that I sensed a certain medical aspect in his character. Perhaps he'd spent so much time in hospital that he'd taken on the air of the surgeon: efficient, tolerant, a little abstracted. And in his case wholly indifferent.)

'Aschau is in part a political re-education centre. I am its director. My name is Köhn. Have you heard of me?'

'No.'

'At Aschau we receive people who stray from the Marxist-Leninist line and we persuade them to rethink.' He watched me the whole time. They all did. 'What made you come here of your own volition?'

'I got the feeling I was straying a bit from the Wilson-Powell line so I thought you could fix me up.'

His eyes were stone-blue and expressionless, the kind of eyes that looked through the glass at guinea-pigs dying of clinically induced cancer.

'I will ask you that question once more.'

He was sitting absolutely still but even so I knew I was right: it wasn't of course Köhn himself that I had recognized, but someone else with these mannerisms and this tone of voice, this way of sitting so absolutely still with the head a fraction on one side and a fraction forward. The walk had been the same, passing through the hall, and if ever he uttered a laugh I knew what sort it would be. But I didn't think Köhn would ever laugh again, even cynically.

'You needn't have asked me at all,' I said. I might as well play it straight and volunteer the information he already had. 'I was sent out from London on a sabotage-investigation job, find out why the Strikers are making holes all over the place.'

He went on watching me and I left it at that because I didn't know how much the *Kamerad Oberst* had told him and even if they've got a fistful of aces there's no point in playing your two of spades.

'How much do you know of the political situation concerning the two Germanies?'

'Is there one? I thought Ulbricht had walled it up.'

He never moved, ever. They might as well have stuck a computer in front of me except that I would have expected this degree of inhuman indifference in a computer: in a live man it struck chill and I decided not to remember the sound I'd heard while we'd been hanging around in the hall.

'I assume you are close to Whitehall.'

'More towards Clapham, really.'

'You decline to admit the extent of your political knowledge and connections.'

'No. They're nil, that's all I mean.'

But he wouldn't just accept that. He was an East German and in East Germany they scratched at their ideology till it bled. If you told them there was a place called Hyde Park where you could stand on an orange-box and shout to hell with the government they'd send you to an asylum for the criminally insane. Perhaps that was why they'd brought me here.

He said: 'Fifteen months ago in his closing address to the Eighth German Party Congress in Berlin, First Secretary Ulbricht took the preliminary steps towards the eventual re-unification of Germany. Since that time there have been overtures made in secret between the two republics. Bonn is expected shortly to withdraw its claim of being the capital of the only legal German state and this will be the signal for overt negotiations to re-establish Germany under a central government whose leaders will be drawn from both sides.'

He paused long enough to let me comment but I didn't say anything because either there'd been a lot going on in both Berlins while everyone else was busy with Czechoslovakia or Köhn was betting on sudden money. You wouldn't find anyone in Whitehall or Clapham for that matter who'd agree that overt negotiations would be the order of the day until the red flag was hoisted at the White House, which didn't seem likely this century. Probably he was just trying to do what I'd done with the big slob: make me correct him.

He put on the other side. 'It is vital that those leaders of the New Germanic State should be neither Eastern lackeys of the Soviet Union nor Western idolaters of the U.S.A. For some time there has been a growing need for the creation of a nucleus of potential government: a consortium capable of assuming control of the New Germany. Such a nucleus now exists.'

Die Zelle.

And bloody Parkis was right again. He didn't know the details but he'd made a blind swipe and come up with the general idea. *Die Zelle* was not only 'existing': it was in gear and on its way, knocking out the opposition on the other side of the wire – Feldmarschall Stöckener and Bundesminister von Eckern *et alia* – and crippling the military structure so that West Germany would have to get out of NATO and surrender any claim to a nuclear role by virtue of an effective air strike-force. Otherwise the U.S.A. would want a lot of say in the election of the New German Government.

Köhn watched me. I still didn't say anything. He'd told me just enough to pitch me into an argument: if I'd had any 'political connections' he knew very well that I'd grab at the chance he was giving me: there were undercover factions in London who'd ally themselves with *Die Zelle* if they knew what he'd just told me and all I'd have to give him were their names. It was no use making them up: he'd check them first. I'd have to get out of Aschau under my own steam or do the other thing.

'You understand my motives in revealing as much as I have, Herr Martin?'

I was going to say yes but one of the lights on the wall-console was winking and he flicked a switch on the internal-communications complex. The voice was very faint in the room: it was one of those whorled-diaphragm speakers that focussed the output and beamed it towards a single listener.

'When did he arrive?'

It's up to the listener to frame his own speech according to whether he wants anyone else in the room to understand. Köhn was indifferent. If I ever left Aschau it would be on his terms.

'Is Schäffer with him?'

It could be the Schäffer they'd thrown out of East Berlin's Humboldt University a month ago. His paper had said that man's thought was the one thing beyond any form of applied philosophy. For 'applied' read 'enforced'. Professor Schäffer would be just the man for a bit of re-education at Aschau.

'Offer him caviar.'

The faint voice went on for a bit and Köhn said: 'Not unless it is essential.' Then he cut the switch and looked at me. 'I asked if you understood my motives, Herr Martin.'

The whole thing was genuine. A man like this didn't have to frighten me with tricks. They'd really brought someone in and he was going to have to fight for his sanity just as I was. So I was getting worried and an idea was forming at the edge of consciousness: the people up there who made inhuman sounds hadn't been brought to Aschau because they were insane. It was the other way round.

I said: 'You want international support for *Die Zelle*. You want me to ferret around the political sewers in London and recruit whatever rats I can find who are willing to work for an outfit that's trying to set up the kind of Germany we had to cut into two so that it couldn't do any more damage. But the kind of new Germany that we all want – its own people included – isn't

128

going to be set up on the dead bodies of men like Stöckener and von Eckern and the thirty-six pilots that *Die Zelle* has murdered so far and it isn't going to be run by people especially qualified to direct a political re-education centre using an asylum for the criminally insane as a front. If you'd like me to elaborate on that I'll do it but I think you get the point.'

One of the other two men moved again uncomfortably. They reminded me of Gühl, the man who had liked marzipan. He had been gun-dependent: these two were Köhn-dependent.

'Your thinking is wrong, Herr Martin, but we may decide at a later date to correct it for you. At Aschau we hold the view that every man is valuable, and that it requires only a little adaptation to put his values to good use. Meanwhile I will ask you to give me full information on the character, functions and personnel of the organization controlling you.'

'Oh come on, be your age.' I was getting fed up.

'You must remember that this is a re-education centre. We are giving you the opportunity of telling us what we require to know without first undergoing re-education. It would save time.'

'I'm in no hurry.'

'Perhaps you underestimate our persuasive abilities?'

'No, I should say they're pretty good.'

'Then why decline to do something voluntarily that you will eventually do under duress? Surely that is a little unrealistic?'

I got out of the chair. He'd given me a lot of info and I wanted to think about it undisturbed and if I stayed here arguing the toss I might forget some of the details that I would need to fit into the pattern before I handed it to Ferris, one fine day.

It never does any good to consider that the only fine day you'll ever get is this one.

'It's no go,' I said.

They all watched me. I took a look at the other two but they weren't interesting. Köhn said:

'Perhaps I can be of help to you by repeating – '

'I don't need help.'

'In your position any man would be glad of it.'

'But not every man. Not this one.'

I was trying to make him specify. If I could get some idea of the actual method it would give me a chance to prepare myself and start combatting it before it began. In London they'd put the 9-suffix against my code-name because I'd twice proved reliable under torture and although I'd stuck it out on those two occasions by the doubtful virtue of sheer bloody pig-headedness it had been Norfolk training that had saved me in the end and a lot of the

Norfolk training deals with the efficacy of psychological prepara-
tion. If you can find out what *kind* of thing you're going into
you've got a chance of containing the natural fear while you're
still fit and in full possession so that when the breath speeds
up and the skin goes cold the mind can be released from the worst
fear of them all: of the unknown.

'I must accept your decision,' he said.

Still wouldn't name it.

'Thank you. Now tell them to heat up the irons.'

He pressed a switch but I couldn't hear anything. It was probably a light-signal outside the room. He said indifferently: 'Our
methods here at Aschau are not those of the Spanish Inquisition.
You will not be molested in any way, of course. Nevertheless you
will shortly give us the information required – that is quite certain'.

The big man came in and Köhn stood up when we left, which
was civil of him.

It was now well after midnight by mental reckoning and most
of the building was quiet, but sometimes I heard voices and a
crack of light showed under some of the doors as I was taken along
the passages. It might have been Cambridge, a few people still
talking in their rooms.

But it was Aschau and I didn't like it because you can't correct
a man's thinking unless you molest him and Köhn said you
could and he ought to know: he'd done it before and was doing it
now to the man who'd made that sound up there and you can
only keep the 9-suffix until you meet someone who knows how
to take it away from you and I believed that Köhn knew how.
He was already applying the worst fear of them all: of the
unknown.

They had double-locked the steel door and I was alone.

They didn't like you to have access to sharp things here and
the beaker above the handbasin was made of soft plastic. I turned
on a tap but it didn't work so I tried the other one but that didn't
work either. Like everything else in East Germany the plumbing
was shoddy. Then I realized this was wrong thinking, just as
Köhn had said: it was mere prejudice. The plumbing was perfectly all right, and I knew why he was so certain that I was going
to tell him all he wanted to know.

Chapter Sixteen

ORDEAL

The scorpion, trapped, will sting itself to death.

Estimation: it would be five days before they dragged me out of here with my tongue rattling. Then Köhn would put his questions and I wouldn't say anything and they would bring me back and leave me alone for another twelve hours and then drag me out again and I wouldn't say anything and they would go on doing it until it became humiliating. I would avoid that. Humiliation.

There were various ways. The window was glazed on the outside of its recess and the bars were inside and level with the wall but I could just reach far enough to smash the glass and get hold of a splinter and use it. The actual flow would take time because of the dehydration and they might be quick getting to me but the chance was good if I went for both wrists and the groin.

The two blankets on the bed were made of processed cellulose pulp stitched inside loose-spun fibre that didn't have any weave to it and even if I could make strips the knots wouldn't hold enough to bear my weight. The bed itself was fixed to the wall with mason's rag-bolts and the handbasin was metal. But they hadn't thought of everything because the electric light worked and when I was ready I could just about bridge the distance between the lamp and the basin, a thumb pressed into the bayonet and a bare foot on the water-pipe.

The other ways might work but I didn't spend too much time thinking about them because they weren't certain. The hand will do what it's told to do and blood-letting and electrocution depend on voluntary manipulation but in a deliberate backward fall with the neck angled the body itself will try to survive: we only have to trip and the hand goes out at once.

Five days before they thought I looked ready, seven or eight before I had to pull the chicken-switch. That was a long time and there might be something I could do as an alternative from going slowly mad with thirst. But I didn't think so. They'd got it all worked out and I wasn't the first one to look round this room and see in everyday things the potential instruments of death.

The air was cold and I checked the radiator. It had lost most of its heat and the tap was open so it looked as if they turned off the main system about midnight. The unit held something like twelve litres of water but the octagonal unions and blanking-plugs were encrusted with paint and it would need a 5-cm spanner to loosen them so I would have to forget it.

I stripped off most of my clothes and dumped them on to the bed for a pillow. The thing was to work out a compromise between staying too warm and getting too cold: normal body-heat produced invisible sweat and I had to hold on to all the fluid I could. Excess cold would drive the blood from the surface and stimulate the kidneys into producing urine. Muscular effort would have to be cut to a minimum but that called for another compromise: there was just a chance that when they came in here again they might make a silly mistake and leave me an opening and I wouldn't be able to take it if the muscles were slack from disuse.

The physical set-up was all right except that the shock-dose of saline in the caviar and beer was already drying the mouth: they had cut down the time-factor by a couple of days. But the problem wasn't only physical. Denied fluid, the body will slowly shrivel to a point where it can no longer support life, but between the onset of thirst and final desiccation there is the effect on the mind. The resolves I was capable of making now could be maintained only so long as I stayed sane.

They were relying on two things. One: that I would be brought to the stage where I would sell the Bureau for a glass of water. No go. We are prepared at any time to do what the scorpion does. Two: that I would lose my reason and become a gibbering traitor. And of this I was afraid. The Bureau and all of those men whose safety depended on the law that secrecy was sacrosanct would remain safe in my keeping until the moment came when sanity was threatened. Before then, and in good time, I would have to blot it all out.

But I was afraid because no man knows when his reason goes: once it has gone he can no longer reason.

The north light came grey from the winter sky through the glass that would soon be smashed.

My one task for the day was to find out if the room were miked because I didn't want them to hear my movements. I found it behind a section of wallpaper just below the ceiling and I tore a wad of pulp from one of the blankets and stuffed it into the gap. Never destroy a mike: it can sometimes be used to carry false information.

The thirst was a worry now and at some time before noon I found myself at the basin making sure the taps were turned on.

Someone might be stupid enough to open the main cock outside the room. I hadn't planned to check on this but it seemed all right, a natural thing to do.

There was some activity in the afternoon: some cars arrived and once I heard a shout as if someone were trying to run free. There was no shooting but the dogs barked a lot just afterwards. Their sound was faint and it reached me through the building, not through the window, so I assumed they were in kennels somewhere at the rear.

The big man came when the light began fading. I was prone on the bunk when he looked through the grille. He opened the door and stood there while the heavy-breasted girl in brogues came in with a waxed picnic-plate. She didn't look at me but just put it carefully across the corner of the basin and went out. There was something about her attitude that gave me the impression that she was afflicted, perhaps deaf-mute.

They were salt-beef sandwiches so it wasn't any good trying to press the moisture out. I didn't even hide them under the bed: unlike thirst, hunger is containable.

In the late evening I got up to make sure the taps were on but didn't actually do it this time. The will-power was coming into its own at this stage: the body had at last recognized that things were serious. They'd no more let someone stupid turn on the water from outside than they'd let him unlock the door. I would have to stop thinking wrongly.

I re-checked before putting the light out: possibility of forcing the metal basin away from the wall and using the brackets or the basin itself to lever the bars apart, possibility of straining the rag-bolts of the bunk and climbing on it to reach the ceiling and break through the lathes and plaster. This was the third floor and there was no support-scaffolding outside the window so the bars weren't too important. There would be nothing higher than the raised width of the bunk to swing up on so a hole in the ceiling wouldn't do any good. The microphone, however muffled, would bring them here to see what I was doing.

Before midnight by mental reckoning they came and woke me from fitful sleep. One stood near me with the black-jack. The other stayed in the doorway and poured water slowly from a jug into a glass and slowly drank it. I turned away as soon as I saw the idea but the sound brought sweat on me, wasting my reserves. Impotence expressed itself in anger surprisingly fast and I had to relax consciously so that I couldn't swing round on them and attack. Any effort of that sort would use up moisture and that was what they wanted.

133

But when they had gone I couldn't sleep again for a long time because of the sound of the water.

Hallucinations began towards the end of the second day, most of them aural. Sometimes they came to the door and opened the grille and poured water for me to hear but sometimes I knew they weren't there, only the noise, because the grille was shut.

My tongue was shrinking now, the mouth a husk. One difficulty was in trying not to review the bodily processes that I knew were going on. Movement could be controlled, and I spent most of the day prone under the window where it was coldest, but breathing had to go on and I knew that every breath was passing moisture from the lungs to waste it on the air. Inactivity and the visual monotony of the walls and ceiling were inducing sleep and I forced wakefulness and concentrated on keeping tidal respiration to a minimum.

They came again at midnight. One filled the glass and offered it to me and I took it at once: the body was avid and the mind careless. Then I smelt petrol and threw it against his face but he was expecting it and ducked and the glass smashed on the wall of the passage outside.

Later I knew they had devised the stratagem so that I should be made to see the glass: being offered it, I wouldn't turn away as I had before. I had been made to see the cool liquidity of what I believed was water and the fact that it was petrol made no difference because I saw it still as they knew I would, shimmering in the dark against my eyes, and it had no smell and it was drinkable, infinitely desirable.

By the evening of the third day I was ready.

The initial shock-dose of saline had advanced the physical process critically and even though inactive, even though for most of the time inert, I had passed more than a gallon of moisture through the skin and lost an added amount from the lungs. The mental process had been advanced by the sight and sound of liquid and by the presence of the taps over the basin. Today I had had to tear the picnic-plate into halves and cover the taps so that they were hidden: because every time I woke it was there that I looked.

I was ready this evening because earlier I had seen a damp patch forming on the wall below the metal basin and heard water trickling. Realizing that it was a leak I began gouging at the plaster but found it was dry, perfectly dry. Memory came back from the far side of the miracle: pipes that are empty cannot leak.

The body could go on for days before it died but the time was shorter for the mind. There had been seven hallucinations during last night and today, three of them visual, and the stage was approaching when I would tell them: *Look, there's water on the wall, his name is Parkis, head of Whitehall 9.* And it would seem reasonable to tell them, reason being gone.

The danger was in proportion to the stake: you can gain more with less to lose. The stake was the Bureau.

In the afternoon I had pulled the wad clear of the microphone and crushed the diaphram. The basin was difficult because I had lost a third of my strength but one of the brackets came away with it and it was a bracket I wanted: the pipes were plastic, not lead. It took an hour to free the bracket from the basin, flexing the bolt until it snapped.

It was a poor weapon but the value of any weapon is increased when it's the only one you have. There was of course no chance of success: none. They always come in pairs and were armed and there were others in the building and the building was itself under guard. Barbed fencing. Whip-lamps. Dogs.

But what I had to do, for pride's sake, before I turned to the final act of blotting it all out, was draw blood.

By midnight they hadn't come.

An hour ago the grille had been opened and closed. I had been standing within three feet of it, close enough to conceal the wall where I'd wrenched the basin away. But they didn't come in, and for this hour I had tormented myself because I could have waited *against* the door and driven the bracket through the grille: an eye for a withered tongue, with luck a death for a death.

The central heating had gone off: the pipes ticked as they contracted, the water cooling, water, cool water.

I left the light burning so that I could see objects that were real; in the dark I could see only fountains shining.

In an hour they came, opening the door quietly without first looking through the grille. The lock turned so slowly that I had to put my hand against the panel and feel the movement of the mechanism, afraid that I imagined it.

When he came in I used my bracket from left to right and starting low to drive upwards and across in a gouging swing to the face and saw surprise and heard his breath snatching as his head jerked back but the swing travelled on and struck nothing and I was off-balance and he knew it and hooked my leg behind the knee. The ceiling span. Somewhere the brain, cool, analytical, computer-quick, wryly reminded the poor fool body that fast

135

action following prolonged inertia was crippled at the start. But we must do our best. He knew his locks: we were down and he worked for my throat and I knew how weak I was but he was worried and trying to speak and I wouldn't listen because they always lied: salt, petrol. Scissors now but he broke it and we rolled over and I worked for the throat again, my left hand flaring, the wound pulling open, rage moving my hands unscientifically and the knee coming up and missing – '*Freund*' – and trying again and missing as he brought his arm across and I felt the lock coming on. '*Freund*,' he grunted again. The light circled. They always lie. The lights flashed and I was under, and water trickled near me, and his breath was sawing, and I could do nothing. Trickling.

He moved very fast and I looked up at him. He stood warily, watching. Water soaked into my hair. It was chill on my scalp. He was holding a flask. It had fallen when we went down, spilling. He nodded, holding the flask for me to take. I got up. The bracket had been lost and I swung an empty hand at the flask but he drew it back, surprised. I stood swaying in the tilting walls and heard warning that I should consider, re-assess, brain-think trying to overcome the animal need to injure the enemy, draw his blood.

Carefully he held the flask towards me again and I considered. There was no petrol smell. This man was alone. They had always come in pairs. The flask was not empty because some had spilled on the floor, puddling beside my head.

He nodded, holding the flask. I turned away. My left hand was growing heavy, the bandage filling. I moved as far as the window and he followed: I could hear him. My breath was like blades in my throat.

'You must drink,' he said and I turned and he was holding the flask. I shook my head. He looked surprised.

Belief began. Belief in water. But if it wasn't, if I tried to drink and found it wasn't, I didn't know what I would do. I would rather not try. Not know.

He seemed to understand and raised the flask and drank, holding it at a distance from his mouth so that I should see that it wasn't a trick. Drops ran down his chin and he wiped them away. He nodded again.

It was an army flask, felt-covered metal with a strap for hitching to the belt. I took it from him and slopped the water into my mouth and tasted it and closed my eyes and drank till there was no more.

*　　*　　*

He seemed to have some small authority because there was a guard in the hall and he told me to wait, and went down the last flight of stairs, speaking to the guard, who turned and went along the lower passage. A door closed in the distance.

The building was quiet. Naked bulbs burned but the spotlights were dark. In a white-walled cellar he threw a high-voltage switch and led me to the top of some steps and into the chill night air.

'Is there more?' I asked. 'More water?'

I had emptied the flask but the thirst raged. It had been like a raindrop on a hot coal.

'Later. There's no time now.'

There were bushes, their leaves black against the sky. The moon swam beyond curdled cloud. He stood close to me, gripping my arm. 'Listen. Go through the fence. Do it quickly: the current is off but I must switch it on again soon. Then go across the ploughed field to the far side. Go straight across. And hurry.'

He pushed me forward.

The earth was frosty under my feet. I shook with cold. The field was wide and I lurched on, letting the weight of my body force me across the ruts. I was free but afraid it might not be true, just as I had been afraid that it might not be water. But the sky was above me and I was alone.

It began when I was halfway across: the distant clamour of alarm-bells, voices and the cry of dogs. Light swept the trees at the far border of the field. Surely I should have learned by now that they always lied.

Chapter Seventeen

THE GRAVE

The thin beams of the whip-lamps pencilled across the trees. The bells had stopped but the dogs voiced their excitement, knowing that they would soon be released because that was what the sound of the bells had always meant.

Perhaps Köhn had altered his decision or his advisers in Neueburg, Linsdorf, Hanover had counselled him that Martin had been operating alone with no back-up cell and was a subject for quick despatch rather than interrogation.

The chill of the earth seeped into me. I lay face down.

A car and then another drove fast to the gates, their sound shifting from left to right, behind me. They were military vehicles, heavy-engined, and the earth flickered under the side-wash of their searchlights.

The policy would be circumspect, a reason forwarded to the relevant authority in the Sozialistische Einheitspartei Deutschlands: a politically dangerous enemy of the State, shot while attempting to escape.

The heavy engines raced, the wheels losing grip on frost-patches. Men shouted. Boots rang on metal footplates.

I began crawling forward along my rut.

Go to him and give him water and then set him running across open land, then alert the guards. Make him trust you or he may go for cover and we don't want difficulties.

For three nights the moon had been bright through the window but now a nimbus layer filtered its light and at moments the land was almost dark. If I got up and ran for cover they might not see me but I suspected the thought: it could be the onset of panic.

More vehicles were on the move.

I need not go, now, in the direction he had told me. But it was the nearest cover. They would know I was going there, to the trees on the far edge of the field, but if I took another direction they would find me sooner: their lights were already closing in at the flank. I crawled faster.

Men shouted to each other in the frosty night.

Then panic came and all I knew was that my hands clawed earth away from under me and pain began spreading from their fingers into my arms as the hard clods broke away and the smell of moisture rose. The sound was the worst: the innermost core of reason, remote from the tumult of disordered thought, heard an animal burrowing.

There is cunning of a kind in panic. Earth was falling across my back, across my legs. My hands shovelled at it, hurrying to make a grave for the living. The only sounds now were the grunt of my own breath and the scrabbling of my own hands: no one was near and this was my world here in the middle of ploughed land and there was work to be done, the quarry to be buried so that the hunters should be deceived as they swung their lights and looked for a running man and gave no thought for worm or mole or this lowly beast whose only shelter was the earth.

Pain swamped my senses and I was lying still, drowning in an ebb and flow of light and dark while the bellows of my lungs reminded me that something was yet alive here, its breath rasping

138

in the hollow of night. Then brilliance swept overhead and lit the ridge of clods my hands had churned. It swept again and I shut my eyes and the panic that had moved me to frenzy now held me paralysed.

Clear thought began. The situation was reviewed. There was nothing more to do: the final decision would now be made by circumstance, by the direction of their lights and the ability of their eyes and the line of their reasoning: they had hunted me before and knew how best to go about it but their very confidence could count against them.

The earth went bright, went dark. The engines throbbed. They turned and backed, sweeping the ploughed area with light, turning and driving on again to probe the trees. Then they sounded to be more distant and the field was dark. And I moved now because the threat in the air had become active: and this danger was the worst. The barking had changed in tone and was more widespread.

They would have given them my coat to scent.

The ruts ran in the direction I had first taken, away from the asylum and towards the thickest of the trees. I knew a road was there; the whole of the ploughed area was ringed. But there was no light showing ahead of me and I scattered earth as I rose and moved at a lurching trot, pitching twice, the horizon spinning, moving on and once halting in an attempt to steady my legs, control them. It was the uneven ground, that was all, the uneven ground: you're far from gone. Get on.

The baying was behind me now and closer.

Light arced across the land to my left and fixed on the low scrub there. The beam appeared to be bouncing but it was my own movement. The ground was bad for running: the frost had crusted the surface and my feet broke through and were caught by the soft earth beneath. I went down again and lay where I fell, listening to the dogs, awareness of their danger blunted by the body's reluctance to get up and go on: it wanted to lie here with its pain and hunger and thirst, to sleep, so as not to feel them.

The dogs must be under the leash still, their handlers making sure it was a true scent before they slipped them, certain of a kill. They were close now.

I was moving again in a drunken run for the dark, for the trees. Brilliance flooded the field's edge and I saw figures grouped. Men's voices mingled with the crying of the dogs.

Somewhere near the trees I fell again, one shoulder hitting the metalled surface of a road. It was very dark here but the shape of the car was visible, massive above me: I had nearly run into it. It had been waiting here with its lights off so that I wouldn't see it. One of its doors swung open.

She said: 'Get in.'

Chapter Eighteen

HELDA

My head was against the floor.

We crawled in the dark and then stopped, backing and waiting. The sound of the dogs was muffled by the bodywork. We turned and there was faint light. I heard the snatch of the universals under the floor. Voices called.

Then we accelerated and turned at speed, pulling up suddenly. The dogs were far away. We started off and settled down to cruising on our way back to the asylum. This was a definite move, a decision, writing off all the uncertainties, and my brain was satisfied and let oblivion come.

'How long have I been out?'

'Half an hour.'

I hadn't moved. My head was still on the floor. I moved and lightning struck through me. I waited before trying again. I asked:

'Where are we?'

'Near Mülhausen.'

'You're lying. You always lie.'

I moved again, my teeth clenched. Faint light was inside the car, pulsing. She got out and opened the door at the back and I felt her hand supporting the side of my head. She knew her stuff: the head is the heaviest bit when you're trying to get off the floor, it's as bad as a ball and chain.

'I don't want your bloody help.'

She went on helping me so I put a lot of effort into it because I wanted to do it for myself. Mülhausen was nowhere near the asylum. It was towards the Frontier. The lying bitch.

I was sitting on the seat, head lolling about. She was trying to keep my head still so that I could drink. She had a flask. They always brought you a flask before they put you through the mincer. After three days they were suddenly lousy with the things. But I drank.

'It's empty,' she said when I'd finished. As if I didn't know. But I suppose she said that because I was still hanging on to it.

'Where are we?'

'Near Mülhausen,' she said carefully. 'Towards the West German Frontier.'

'Leave that alone.' She was trying to find the end of the bandage among all the mess. It was humiliating. I pulled my hand away.

'Clench it,' she said. 'Keep it clenched. You've been losing blood.

'What the hell've you brought me here for? Give the dogs a longer run?'

The light from the dashboard had stopped pulsing. She was watching my face. 'How long can you hold out?'

'A long time. I was thirsty, that's all. Who are you?'

'My name is Helda.'

'I mean who *are* you?'

But one or two pointers were presenting themselves for my inspection. When I had got into the car she'd crawled in the dark at first so by the time she'd put her lights on she'd have been some distance from where the dogs were milling about at the end of the scent-track. Then she'd backed and waited, floodlighting the field, keeping up the search like the rest of them. Then she'd driven off hard for the next search-area.

The water was cold in my stomach. My whole body was drinking there. I said:

'You'll be missed by now. Better shove on.'

She was watching me attentively. 'When did you last eat?'

She knew when I'd last eaten. 'Three days ago.' Maybe she didn't.

'Nothing since then?'

'You think I fancy salt-beef sandwiches? I'm used to caviar.'

The bronze eyes lit and softened and suddenly she looked as she had when I'd thought about her as a change from thinking about blotting it all out. It was relief, that was all. I was a mess but it sounded as if the inside of my head was still operating and obviously there were things we had to do.

'Drink this.'

Plastic bottle. 'What is it?'

'Glucose and milk.'

I took it and she unscrewed the top. Compared with the water the milk was warm: she'd had it in the pocket of her flying-coat. While I drank slowly she left me and got behind the wheel. I climbed out and dumped myself in the front beside her partly to see if I could do it and partly so we wouldn't have to shout. But she didn't say anything until we were through Mülhausen and into the minor roads.

'I'm taking you to the Frontier.'

'Out on a limb, aren't you?'

'It's my affair.'

Shivering had set in and she noticed it: 'I couldn't bring your coat.'

'No. The dog-handlers had it.'

I still heard the baying and would hear it for a long time. Delayed shock was trying to start but it wouldn't have much luck because I was too interested in what was going on. After a while I said: 'We haven't got long.'

'It wasn't just bad organization,' she said. 'My duty was to pick up Gühl. They were waiting for his report on the Benedikt situation. I couldn't do anything except hand you over. I couldn't even talk in the car because of the driver. I could only plan to get you away as soon as I could do it. That should have been much sooner but the sky was clear until tonight and they would have got you before you'd gone a yard. I'm sorry.'

'You're taking a chance even now.'

'But it's at least a chance.'

She drove deftly: her nerves showed only in the way she spoke, a few brief phrases broken by short intervals of silence. I said: 'Who are you with?'

'No one you would know. We had a cell established in Zagreb.'

I waited but that was all. I couldn't ask anything else because it wouldn't be ethical and anyway she wasn't going to tell me anything more than we would both need to share for the sake of security. But I thought I had it: there'd been someone in Zagreb recently who'd had to do a bunk and it had stirred things up a lot. Two people had shown up in London soon afterwards and we'd vetted them in case they had any value for the Bureau. All we'd learned was that the Zagreb base was blown and that three of their regional cells were cut off. It happens a lot: it's bound to. It can't happen to the established networks: the American C.I.A. has a hundred thousand personnel and you could drop a multi-megaton buster down their chimney and no one would get cut off anywhere because their outfit is fully diversified, but there are thousands of pint-sized private-enterprise groups working the clock round from Leningrad to Lisbon and they haven't resources wide enough to cushion the crunch if it comes.

'You did pretty well,' I said.

'No. We – '

'I mean it's not everyone who can fix up a secret-police cover and live too long.' I didn't want her to explain how pretty well she hadn't done. It can happen to the best of them: they've nowhere to go once their base is blown and the best of them just go on operating in the hope that somehow they can bring it off alone. But they can't do that if they come down to the broken reeds among their number. People like Benedikt.

'We were cut off,' she said and there was a sag in her voice because she was only now recognizing the defeat that she'd refused to face before.

'It can happen to anyone. But why send a man like him to a place like Hanover when you had at least two other people right inside London?'

She looked at me and away again. I was knowing too much. That wasn't awkward: it was just embarrassing. She said in a moment: 'I couldn't trust them.'

That fitted. Benedikt had broken but he hadn't sold out. He'd left them safe.

'But you didn't drop the idea. I mean of calling on London.'

It wasn't the first time a group had signalled for help. A lot of them were the nuclei of resistance cells and refugee organizations and even though times had changed and the hot war had gone cold they were still of the generation that once had nothing to sustain them in the twilight of the attics and the cellars and the boarded-up cupboards but the voice among the static prefaced by the four notes of the V-sign: *This is London.* But it was the first time my own Bureau had mounted a mission and sent out an agent within hours of a contact. We get a lot of contacts and most of them are duff but just as soon as Lovett tipped us off about an imminent Striker crash I was lying on my back on top of a chalk quarry with that very aeroplane performing overhead. And there'd been *nothing* to go on. Lovett himself hadn't known who the contact was.

I suppose people loathe Parkis because he's always so bloody right.

She said: 'If London couldn't do anything, you'd tell me now, wouldn't you?'

'Yes.'

We were running through flat country: a few hedgerows and then nothing but the far horizon. The car slewed sometimes across frost but she held it well enough.

'It wasn't bad organization,' she said and I knew she was worried about it. 'They must have gone to have another look at you soon after you'd left. I was counting on at least one hour before that happened. We couldn't – '

143

'Look, I'm here and I'm not thirsty any more. Well for God's sake.'

'All right.'

'Did you send Benedikt across on a specific mission or was he just meant to check on the Hanover cell?'

'He was to take over the Striker operation.'

Of course. So he'd known when the next one would crash. And had told Lovett. I said: 'Can you fill me in on Köhn?'

The roads were narrower here and the tarmac was broken in places. The terrain was taking on the wasteland look of the Frontier Zone.

'Distinguished flying record, the Iron Cross as a lieutenant, 1944. He was cut off after a crash-landing near Poznan a year later and taken prisoner by the Soviet troops in that area. He never saw his family again and he didn't know at the time that his wife was killed in the bombing of Cologne. When they released him he began working for privileges as a pro-communist – '

'Why didn't he go back before 1961? He could have. There was a child, wasn't there?'

She said reflectively: 'I think it may have been his pride, or – '

'Oh I see, yes.' At that time his face would have been still in the healing stages and frightening to a small boy.

We began slowing and she switched to low-beam. The dark mass of pines loomed on our left and at its fringe were the trees I had memorized as markers on our way across.

Time was so short.

I said: 'You're going straight back?'

'As soon as I know you're through safely.' She slowed to a crawl and drove on sidelights between hedges of thorn. 'They'll have widened the search by now and I'll join them.'

I didn't ask what the risk was: she would have been absent for two hours. I said: 'Who are the people we have to deal with? The ones at the top with Köhn?'

'There are others. Gröss, Langmann and Schott. Langmann is based in East Berlin. The others are at Aschau.'

'Langmann – what's his cover?'

'Secretary of Trade Agreements in the S.E.D.'

'They're the all-highest? Those four?'

'If they were brought down,' she said, 'the whole of *Die Zelle* would collapse.'

She turned off the side-lights before the thorn gave way to scrubland and we went forward at a walking-pace through the faint light from the sky. She said:

'Köhn, Gröss and Schott go by road to Berlin once every month for conference with the political re-education secretariat. They are normally escorted by one military vehicle.'

'Oh really.'

'I tried,' she said.

'Of course.'

'There are only three of us and there's so little we can do. Aschau is a network of microphones and every second man is an informer.'

'You've done well enough to survive.' Aschau was a Chinese Box: within an asylum for the criminally insane was the legitimate but undercover political re-education complex. Within that, *Die Zelle*. Within that, Helda's group, a potential detonator.

'Survival isn't enough.'

'It's kept open the way in. You know that.'

She cut the engines and we coasted, bumping over rough ground where the track ended. Then we stopped.

I said: 'If my people decide to have a go they'll want to look over Aschau. I mean as well as fix the convoy on the Berlin run. There might be some confusion when it all hots up so we'll have to arrange a code-intro.'

We couldn't see much of each other now because the facia lamp was out. We spoke more quietly.

'Might you be there?' she asked.

'No. It's not in my field.'

In a moment she said: 'What is your name?'

'Quiller.'

Slowly she said: 'Quiller. Tell them we shall use that.'

'All right.'

'We shall use the English pronunciation.'

'Yes.' There were a few German words that would sound similar if the 'u' were spoken as 'v'.

We were accommodating visually to the dim light and I could see the dark shape of her mouth and the glow of her eyes. I could feel her warmth. I said:

'You'll have been absent for two hours. How big is the risk?'

'It's calculated.'

Köhn would give the orders and they would arrange it discreetly and the glow and the warmth would be gone.

'Come across with me now. You'd be given immediate asylum.'

She moved her head, looking through the wind-screen at the distant posts where the wire ran. 'No. It would mean letting them down. My friends. And if your people decide to go over there I shall try to have material available. Documents, rosters, everything they'll have come for.' She looked at me again. 'I tried to

145

get your papers back, and the key-plan of the mines. It wasn't possible.'

'I took bearings.' The chill air flowed in as I opened my door. 'Go straight back.'

'I shall wait until I know.'

Sharply I said: 'There's no point. If I make a mistake there'll be nothing you can do. Go straight back.'

'Very well.'

Looking in at her I said: 'We met late, didn't we?'

'Yes.'

I shut the door and began walking.

I was more than halfway across before the tension got so bad that I had to rest. The danger was in the need to concentrate: there comes a time when the mind refuses further discipline and argues that luck will get you through. Marksmen at the range find that their aim deteriorates after a certain point and they put it down to fatigue but it isn't the whole answer.

There was no deliberate intention to rest: suddenly I was lying on my back, face to the curdled clouds, eyes closed, my nervous reserves already plundered – I lay down without caution, not caring whether or not my head was blown off.

Eyelids flickering. Posts and stanchions, a forest of them reaching to infinity, charred shadows against the ashen frost – 32 *LG-RR/4/45/42SILCB-T/6/45/5* – *Bearing 3: 2nd post Left of Guard-hut to line with Right edge of Ruin, 4 paces, 45° to Bearing 4: 2nd stanchion from 1st post Left of Central Bush to line with Tree, 6 paces, 45° to Bearing 5* – the earth cold against my back, my spine a perfectly articulated thread of life lying at an unknown angle among perfectly ordered points of potential death, a man seeking on ancient principle his own survival, men seeking by remote artifact his extermination.

Who are you?

Quiller.

I mean who *are* you?

This bit of gristle cast up in no man's land where no man safely goes, nursing a bandage full of blood and the high ambition of crawling through a wire where the cows come to scratch their backs and where the hemispheres of the planet Earth divide. The sky flickering. Get up. Get on your bloody feet.

53RT-LF6/45/61S2LCB to Bearing 7.

Keep still.

'Poor sod.'

Still. Reference shifting: second marker seventh series had

doubled. There was no tree there before. R3-check and make four paces.

'You'd not think it were worth it, would you?'

Voices low. Assimilate new situation and discount alien markers and proceed. Prominence – *watch it*! Feel it. Feel its edge. Stone.

It had brought the sweat out.

'He's not the only one that's tried. It must be bad over there.' The gleam of their guns.

To line with Left edge of Guard hut, 4 paces.

But I was weakening now and the second marker swayed and I couldn't get a true fix on the background reference but it was no good flaking out again because the next time I'd fall on top of one and I didn't want that, all I wanted was sleep.

'Come on, son, you'll do it yet.'

I suppose so. I suppose so. *Bearing* 10.

The hiss of the frost underfoot, 6 *paces*.

The wire. The barbs bent under with pliers. Now don't fall over. There's no need.

'Are you – are you blokes Rhine Army?'

'Christ – he's English!'

One of them caught me.

Chapter Nineteen

FINAL APPROACH

They put me in the back of their Jeep and one of them slung his greatcoat round me. They were already calling up base as we drove off. The wind cut cold. I shouted against it.

'I left a car here. Can I pick it up?'

'You what?' They talked together. 'You can't drive it because we can't authorize you, see? And we can't drive it because no one can authorize us, get it? So I should just sit tight and look happy. We shan't be long.'

They were in good spirits. It wasn't often they picked anyone off the wire.

At the B.A.O.R. unit a captain questioned me and went into his office next door to use the phone. I could hear most of it through the pinewood partition. *A very odd bod indeed. Thorough bad shape but lucid enough. Is Mister Bates there?*

A corporal brought me a cup of tea.

I dunno, frankly. He wants to talk to someone in Hanover. Yes. Thing is, do we let him?

I burnt my lips but went on drinking just to feel the heat. The corporal was passing on the news somewhere outside: *He's in there now. Caught him on the Strip. Eh? No, English. Honest!*

Fair enough. We'll hold him for you.

Boots in the passage. 'Thomson!'

'Sir?'

'Bring some tea for this chap, soon as you can.'

'He's got some, sir.'

'Fair enough.'

The door opened. 'You can phone Hanover but we have to listen in, that do you?'

He took me into his office and I gave him the number. We waited for the connection. Tall, clean, pink-faced, very interested, a boyish smile. 'The last customer we had was two months ago. I mean a live one.' That was how they must come to see the 'Strip': as a wire where birds perched, some of them falling.

When the phone rang he used the extension, watching me the whole time as I talked.

'Sapphire.'

'Needle.' He listened for bugs. 'All right.'

I said: 'Company.' Third party this end.

'Understood.'

'I'm in B.A.O.R. Bucholz. Get me out, will you?'

'This time of night?'

He was giving himself time to think. The Rhine Army wouldn't pick anyone up unless they were right in the Zone.

'Wake people up,' I told him.

'Yes. Which way are you facing?'

'Home.' He wanted to know if I were going across or coming back.

The young captain tapped my arm: 'It's getting a little obscure. I'm afraid I'll have to ask you to – '

'All right,' I said.

'Anything for me?' Ferris was asking.

'Practically the lot.'

'Oh yes?' He was very good at not sounding galvanized. 'Anything for London?'

'Not yet.'

'I ought to give them at least a rough – '

'Look, stuff London. Just get me out. I want one more day.'

'Where?'

'Linsdorf. Do I need smoke out?'

148

'No. We fixed that.'

The captain reached across and cut us off. His smile was rather strained. 'I do apologize, but you see my position. Most of that was in verbal code and I've already stuck my neck out letting you phone at all.'

I gave him the receiver.

'I appreciate that.' The heat was off now and the need for sleep was urgent. 'Appreciate it a lot. Don't worry, there'll be no kick-back.' Up to Ferris, the rest of the night.

'That's fine. But the thing is, you could be Commander Crabb or someone.'

'He's got brown eyes, didn't you know?'

They woke me just before dawn and I let them take me along to the sick-bay to get the hand re-stitched.

'There's not so much room left for making new holes, that's the trouble. What have you been doing?'

'I had to go on all fours for a bit.'

'Taking pots, were they?' The M.O. laughed gustily. They all knew where the 'very odd bod' had been. It was a routine patrol unit and I was as good as the telly.

The captain took me back to his office.

'Well I'm not quite sure what's going on but we've had a call through and my orders are to release you and offer limited facilities.' He sounded frustrated: he wasn't averse to letting me go but he realized that he would never know who it was who had gone. 'Perhaps you'd give me some idea as to what facilities you need.'

I didn't ask for much: some biscuits, a duffle-coat, some petrol and a ride in the Jeep as far as the ruined military depot.

The 17M was still there, stuck in the bush, and they filled the tank while I scraped the frost off the wind-screen. The tank had been split on the blind run from Neueburg and I didn't want to go dry. I made sure the engine would start before I let them go, then while it warmed I stood looking east across the wire and the flat grey land beyond. The light seeped from a cold sky and there were crows about: it was morning, and I had a warm coat with biscuits in a pocket and I hoped the night had gone well for her, as it had gone for me.

The front wing rattled but the roads smoothed out when I cleared the Zone and headed north towards Linsdorf.

Clive? This is George. Listen, something's come up and we'd rather like your help. Well apparently there's one of *those* chaps – you know? – struck a spot of trouble in Western Germany. Yes

Name's Martin and he's officially attached to the Accidents Investigation Branch working at an air-base called Linsdorf. Now this is what seems to have cropped up, you listening hard?

I ate the biscuits slowly, a crumb at a time.

Number Three? This is Beacon Nine. Will you be in Bonn tonight? Well you'll see General Schmidl, obviously. Subject: an Englishman, Walter Martin, has become wanted for murder since early hours this morning. All we need is that the good *Herr General* is tipped off that his K.P. branch is wasting its time: Martin was not, repeat not, responsible. They'll thus avoid unproductive search tactics. M'm? If it could be done officially I wouldn't be asking you, would I? No, we're relying on Schmidl's confidence in our integrity and that should suffice. Finally, if the Kriminal-polizei require the said Martin as witness at a later date, we guarantee his availability. Now I'll give you what details I have.

My left hand was no more than numb beneath its fresh anal-gesic dressing. I had slept for nearly three hours at the Rhine Army unit but there was a certain amount of natural dope trying to put me out again because I was still about twelve hours on the debit side. I kept all the windows down.

Liebermann? I have some confidential information for you. I can give you nothing of its source but I would suggest that you accept it as most reliable. Further, I would invite you to take such action as will become clear to you when you know the facts. Please listen to me carefully.

Neueburg lay to the east now and I passed the turning, making directly north. Soon afterwards I saw a cruising police patrol and felt gratitude to Ferris. My journey to Linsdorf and my business there would have been impossible or at best very difficult in smoke conditions, but the heat had been turned off Martin and I could go where I pleased. It was one of the things a director in the field was expected to do for his agent but I felt good about Ferris because there were those who wouldn't have kept up the pressure on London until something was done.

I approached Linsdorf just before 10.00 a.m. A Striker SK-6 was going into circuit after take-off and the smell of kerosene tainted the draught from the windows.

He was in a bad way even before I told him, his nerves in his eyes, couldn't keep still, the short laugh more cynical than ever.

'We were wondering where you'd gone,' he said.

In this kind of confrontation they are not always so vulnerable and it surprised me but it was too late to change tactics and I whipped it on him right away.

'I've been at Aschau.'

We were alone in his quarters. I had noted his service revolver among some gear on a chair and I was standing where I could block him if he went for it.

Reaction wasn't total. I hadn't expected it to be. All he knew now was that I was a bit more than an aviation psychologist attached to the A.I.B. head tilted, a degree sideways and a degree forward. He knew who I was not; he didn't know who I was.

'Yes?'

I said: '*Die Zelle* is finished.' But of course he would need more than that. He would want proof. 'Köhn, Gröss, Langmann, Schott, all of them. Finished.'

Total reaction now, much earlier than I'd expected because he still didn't have any proof. But within half a minute I hardly recognized him: the shock had aged his face and sharpened its resemblance to his father's.

'Thank God,' he said.

I had to think about that. The unexpected was coming up all the time and I tried to recognize familiar facts but there was only one with relevance. Nitri had said in the car: *He's enormously brave.* For a man with his record of courage his nerves had needed a lot of tranquillizing: a woman a night, so they said.

Then I got it.

'Pushing you too far, were they?'

He said nothing. His face had lost all colour and his eyes were vacant: in the way of a drowning man he was reviewing his life and if I had spoken again he wouldn't have heard or understood.

After a long time he said numbly: 'Yes. I tried to tell him. But he said a part of the new Germany was in my care. That was what he said.'

'In your care?' I was getting fed up. 'And thirty-six pilots, one after the other – were they in your care too?'

Abstractedly: 'That was Wagner.'

'Oh really? Nothing to do with you? Christ, I wouldn't want your conscience, Röhmhild.'

Wagner wasn't much surprise. I'd already checked on him, coming into the air-base. He'd left here two days ago. Rotational duties: he'd be down at Hankensbüttel now, the next one round the ring.

'I did it for him.'

'What? Oh, for Köhn. You're all the same – you can never do anything for yoursleves, there's always got to be some kind of a tin god telling you what to do. Then you'll do anything. When did they tell you, the Röhmhilds?' Because it must have been like that.

'When I was fifteen.'

'Well that was a bloody silly thing to do.'

Puberty is no time to tell someone he's got a genuine father lost on the other side of a lot of barbed wire: he'll want to find him. I wondered if Köhn would ever have allowed that. He'd had no choice. The Röhmhilds had thought it was the right thing to do.

I said: 'When did you first meet him?'

'On my nineteenth birthday.' But his answers weren't coming as fast as that. He spent a lot of time staring at nothing. 'I went across the Wall on a holiday pass and tried not to come back but he made me.'

'Was that when it happened?' He stared at me, trying to connect. 'Was that when he offered you the sacred task of assisting in the re-creation of the beloved Fatherland and all that balls?'

Something like anger came into his eyes: I'd kicked half a temple over and there has to be a place to pray in when you worship a god. *Distinguished flying record, the Iron Cross as a lieutenant*, so forth. And a face to show for it: the face of the mutilated martyr. They'd had young Röhmhild-Köhn across a barrel.

'It was later. A year later.'

'What was your job? Recruiting Wagner?'

'Yes.'

More than that. For the past year he'd been *Die Zelle*'s contact inside the Luftwaffe, monitoring pilot-reactions, listening to the A.I.B. wreckage-analysts, checking on their West German counterpart team, passing it all through the wire with people like Gühl as a courier. Linsdorf was the main base where the Striker-crash investigations were going on.

'How much longer were you going to keep it up?'

'It was not in my hands, after Wagner had worked out a way to –'

'Oh all right, but you had all the information, didn't you, you knew who was next on the list? What was it? Drugs? Hypnosis? A nerve-gas?'

'I don't know.'

'Of *course* you know!'

'He didn't tell me!'

'*Damn* your eyes – how was it *administered*?'

His head had swung away as if I'd hit him. From somewhere he was trying to rescue reason and re-arm himself but there was

152

no defence against what I had told him: that *Die Zelle* was finished. The divine orders from the god in the temple had been to engineer the death of young men like himself who flew the same plane and lived the same life, and his subscription to opposing loyalties had finally cut him in two, just as all Germany was cut.

If I stopped now I'd never get it from him. 'What was his *method*? Wagner's *method*?' Because London wouldn't go in immediately: she'd said the Berlin run was normally scheduled for the fifteenth of every month.

'It was a tablet.'

'Where? Where did he – '

'In the tube of sedatives – '

'Oh Christ, as simple as that?' They were out there rebuilding whole aeroplanes. 'What was it, the fifth in the tube, the sixth? How many sedative doses before the big kick, Röhmhild? One every flight? How many flights a day? How many days?'

He stood shivering and I turned away. He didn't have to answer: the answer was on the map, the ring on the map. Wagner spent an average of five days at every main Striker base. His duties were rotational and death was rotational: Russian roulette. He would alter his time-pattern so that he would never be present at any given base when a crash happened. Pick the next man and get out, just as you light a fuse.

And the stuff could be anything, a quick-acting depressant using the normal effects of high-altitude and oxygen-breathing as a catalyst: that would be essential because they had to come down hard enough to make analysis impossible. Ferris: *You saw that crash so you can imagine what the pilot looks like afterwards.* Quick-acting and short duration: I had asked Philpott what attitude the Striker would adopt if the pilot lost control and hadn't switched to automatic. *Nose down, four or five degrees.* From sixty thousand feet, all the way into the ground.

He was standing looking out of the window but I knew that nothing was familiar to him any more.

'How long have you been at Linsdorf?'

'Six months.'

'Got a transfer here did you?'

He said nothing more. But it was six months ago when the West German analysts and the A.I.B. had set up Linsdorf as the centre of their operations. The eye and the ear of *Die Zelle* had requested transfer.

'Who's next, Röhmhild?'

He didn't answer, perhaps didn't hear. His silence gave me time to think and suddenly I knew that I was missing something important: I didn't know what it was but the natural thing happened and my thoughts focused on the one area still unexplained. Röhmhild had been so vulnerable when I had come here and I had assumed it was due to the strain of standing by and doing nothing while they came out of the sky one after another at Günzburg, Spalt, Laubach, Linsdorf –

'*Röhmhild.*' Wagner gone. Rotational. The taint of kerosene in the draught from the windows. '*Who is next?*' I swung him round and his face opened to the shock of the attack: he'd even forgotten I was here, and forgotten why.

'Artur Boldt.'

Geschwaderkommodore, Linsdorf. Now airborne.

I dragged at the door and began running and was halfway to the control tower when I heard the shot but kept on going, the odd thought flashing to mind that Nitri was off the hook now. The pilots heard it from the crew-room and came out to see what was happening and one of them called to me but I went on running. Concrete apron, dry ice in the shallows, a flight of steps, steel banister, the door.

They were surprised to see me. Green glass filtering the light. I told them to get him down, do it *now*, catch him before he reached his operational ceiling (because it could be a part of the trick, normal effects of high altitude as a catalyst), said I was with A.I.B. and we'd located the fault because they weren't too quick but that one worked all right and they started calling him up.

I leaned on the edge of the console, irritated at being out of breath, a lot of steps, fair enough, but I must be getting old.

Geschwaderkommodore, Geschwaderkommodore. Antworten Sie bitte!

Crackling static.

Natural selection on Wagner's part, I supposed. The *Geschwaderkommodore* was a danger. We'd all been standing there just after Paul Dissen had done his bang and Boldt had said *it's not the plane, it's the pilot.*

Geschwaderkommodore. Hören Sie? Antworten Sie bitte!

And Wagner had been there when Boldt had said that. Little Wagner, their shepherd, their saviour: *You have a theory, I know.* And Boldt had said: *Several.*

Befehl – Sofortiger Rückflug zur Staffel!

The sky looked empty through the green glass.

Hören Sie? Hören Sie?

Just airborne when I'd reached the gates. Fifteen twenty minutes with Röhmhild. Take less than that to reach the ceiling but then he might not be climbing the whole time, it depended on what exercise he –

Befehl übermittelt!

Signal received.

The controller nodded to me and I went out and down the steps. There were some pilots and one or two of the ground staff in a group outside the door of Röhmhild's quarters and an ambulance was nosing in.

I didn't recognize him at first, glasses glinting and straw-coloured hair bobbing as he walked. I hadn't expected him.

'What's come up?' I asked.

He was gazing cautiously around, typical of him, and some other people were coming past to see what was going on, so he walked me as far as the perimeter road. Of course I knew why he'd come: he'd been in signals, so forth. He said:

'I had to tell London straight away and they said I ought to make contact. What's that ambulance for?'

'Tell them what?'

He gave me his quiet nervous-breakdown look. 'You said you were home and dry when you phoned me from Rhine Army. Well are you?'

The sky was still empty. My eyes were getting tired staring up at it. I said: 'They think I was going to lose the whole thing down a drain or something at the last minute? Bloody London for you.'

'Well they're anxious, you know. They didn't expect you to crack it inside a week.' His pale head was turning like a radar. 'What's the ambulance for?'

'Bloke shot himself. The classic Prussian *kaputt*.'

A whisper in the air, very high, like the one over Westheim. I listened to it.

'Any immediate action?' He was being very good, very off-hand, but he knew the ferret was out through the far end and he was keen to see the rabbit.

'Not really.' I shielded my eyes. It hadn't been so high as it had sounded: the shape was already forming in the winter haze, drifting into the final approach. I said: 'What's the date?'

'Fifth.' He'd seen the plane now.

'There's some local stuff. The bloke over there was in it but I got what I wanted out of him. There's a man called Wagner you'll need to bring in and there's a clockmaker's in Neueburg that wants cleaning out.'

'A what?'

'A clockmaker's.' I wished he'd go away. I wanted to watch the plane come down because there'd been nothing I could do about it at Westheim. 'People need clocks, don't they? So people have to make them.'

Touch and bounce, then it tilted and slid very fast down the strip, the brakes coming on, slowing at the north end, turning.

'Not pretty, are they?' Ferris said.

'That one is.' It was coming in to the hangars and I turned away. 'But the big job is an ambush over the other side, couple of vehicles on the move between a place called Aschau and Berlin. And a political re-education centre to clean out. The vehicles go up every month on the fifteenth so you've got ten days, that's all right. Moondrop job, half a dozen assault specialists. How will Parkis do it, with internationals or what?'

'He'll probably hand it to Bonn. It's really their pigeon.'

I turned once and had a last look. Humped, ugly, bow-legged, stinking of kerosene. We walked on again.

'Because I want London to send me with them.'

'It's not your field.'

'Just for the ride, that's all.'

He was glinting at me sideways, hair all over the place, quite alarmed. A shadow executive mustn't ever go and play with the rough boys down the street, it says so in the rules.

'They wouldn't let you. Anyway you've had enough by the look of things.'

'Listen, Ferris.' I was getting fed up: I wanted a bit of sleep that was all. 'I cracked this one inside a week, didn't I? My credit's good, for once. So you're going to fix it for me, all right? I mean that.'

Behind us the jet whined away to silence.

'I'll do what I can. Someone over there, is there?'

'That's right.'

Helen MacInnes

Born in Scotland, Helen MacInnes has lived in the United States since 1937. Her first book, *Above Suspicion*, was an immediate success and launched her on a spectacular writing career that has made her an international favourite.

'She is the queen of spy-writers.' *Sunday Express*

'She can hang up her cloak and dagger right there with Eric Ambler and Graham Greene.' *Newsweek*

Above Suspicion

Assignment in Brittany

Decision at Delphi

The Double Image

Horizon

I and My True Love

Message from Málaga

Neither Five Nor Three

North from Rome

Pray for a Brave Heart

The Salzburg Connection

The Venetian Affair

 *Fontana Books*

Eric Ambler

A world of espionage and counter-espionage, of sudden violence and treacherous calm; of blackmailers, murderers, gun-runners—and none too virtuous heroes. This is the world of Eric Ambler. 'Unquestionably our best thriller writer.' *Graham Greene*. 'He is incapable of writing a dull paragraph.' *Sunday Times*. 'Eric Ambler is a master of his craft.' *Sunday Telegraph*

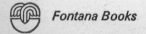 *Fontana Books*

H. H. Kirst

Sometimes very funny, often bitingly satirical, Hans Hellmut Kirst's novels describe Germany and the Germans, from the Nazi era to the present day. 'Kirst's oblique, deadpan gaze is deeply revealing, deeply compassionate.' *Sunday Times*

A Time for Scandal

The Revolt of Gunner Asch

Gunner Asch Goes to War

The Return of Gunner Asch

What Became of Gunner Asch

Officer Factory

The Night of the Generals

The Wolves

 *Fontana Books*

Fontana Books

Fontana is best known as one of the leading paperback publishers of popular fiction and non-fiction. It also includes an outstanding, and expanding, section of books on history, natural history, religion and social sciences.

Most of the fiction authors need no introduction. They include Agatha Christie, Hammond Innes, Alistair MacLean, Catherine Gaskin, Victoria Holt and Lucy Walker. Desmond Bagley and Maureen Peters are among the relative newcomers.

The non-fiction list features a superb collection of animal books by such favourites as Gerald Durrell and Joy Adamson.

All Fontana books are available at your bookshop or newsagent; or can be ordered direct. Just fill in the form below and list the titles you want.

FONTANA BOOKS, Cash Sales Department, G.P.O. Box 29, Douglas, Isle of Man, British Isles. Please send purchase price, plus 8p per book. Customers outside the U.K. send purchase price, plus 10p per book. Cheque, postal or money order. No currency.

NAME (Block letters) _____

ADDRESS _____

_____

_____